Elizabeth Gail and the Secret Box

Hilda Stahl

Tyndale House Publishers, Inc., Wheaton, Illinois

Dedicated with love to
Ed, Vera, Bob, Steve, Dan, and Kevin Stahl

The Elizabeth Gail Series
1 *Elizabeth Gail and the Mystery at the Johnson Farm*
2 *Elizabeth Gail and the Secret Box*
3 *Elizabeth Gail and the Teddy Bear Mystery*
4 *Elizabeth Gail and the Dangerous Double*
5 *Elizabeth Gail and Trouble at Sandhill Ranch*
6 *Elizabeth Gail and the Strange Birthday Party*
7 *Elizabeth Gail and the Terrifying News*
8 *Elizabeth Gail and the Frightened Runaways*
9 *Elizabeth Gail and Trouble from the Past*
10 *Elizabeth Gail and the Silent Piano*
11 *Elizabeth Gail and Double Trouble*
12 *Elizabeth Gail and the Holiday Mystery*
13 *Elizabeth Gail and the Missing Love Letters*
14 *Elizabeth Gail and the Music Camp Romance*
15 *Elizabeth Gail and the Handsome Stranger*
16 *Elizabeth Gail and the Secret Love*
17 *Elizabeth Gail and the Summer for Weddings*
18 *Elizabeth Gail and the Time for Love*

Cover and interior illustrations by Kathy Kulin

Juvenile trade paper edition

Library of Congress Catalog Card Number 78-63097
ISBN 0-8423-0740-0, paper
Copyright 1979 by Hilda Stahl
Printed in the United States of America

4   5   6   7   8   9   10   95   94   93   92   91   90

Contents

ONE
Surprise in the mail

Libby clutched her English book tightly as she raced down the long driveway. She felt like shouting and laughing, but she had to use every bit of her strength. Today she had to beat Ben to the house. She could hear him close behind her. She knew Susan would be right behind him, and Kevin behind her. For almost a week they'd been racing to the house after they got off the school bus. Ben always won. But not today! Libby was going to beat him today!

Libby caught sight of Ben beside her, which sent her into a fresh burst of speed. She knew if she cut across the snowy yard and around the end of the house, she would beat him for sure. But one of the rules was that you stay on the long driveway to get around to the garage and to the back door. And she wouldn't cheat. None of them did.

Just then a wild honking filled the air. Libby's heart skipped a beat. Goosy Poosy was joining the race. Just so he stayed away from her! She did not want him flying against her and knocking her down. She wasn't really afraid of him; well, maybe just a little.

Libby spotted the pet goose just as Ben whizzed around her to the back door. He laughed triumphantly.

"I almost beat you, Ben," said Libby, her hazel eyes sparkling happily. "Maybe tomorrow."

"Maybe," he said, holding his hands out to Goosy Poosy. The goose rubbed his long neck up and down Ben's arms.

"You're sure getting fast," said Susan, smiling as she stopped beside Libby. Susan had long red-gold hair which was covered by the hood of her blue jacket. She was almost a head shorter than Libby, even though she was the same age.

"Hi, Goosy Poosy," said Kevin as he slid to a stop. He punched his glasses up on his nose, then bent to stroke the white goose.

Slowly Libby rubbed Goosy Poosy's long neck. How long would it take before she didn't have to force herself to touch him?

"I'm glad you aren't scared to death of Goosy Poosy anymore," said Ben, smiling at Libby.

Libby felt warm all over at the words and smile. She smiled at Ben. She liked his red hair and hazel eyes. He was always so nice to her even when she wasn't being very nice.

Susan walked beside Libby through the door. "Libby, I heard Brenda Wilkens making fun of you on the bus," said Susan as she pulled off her warm jacket. She flipped her hair over her slender shoulders. "Try not to let her make you feel bad."

"I guess she doesn't believe an aid kid is good enough to be her friend," said Libby, peeling off her jacket. "I wanted to tell her that I would like to be friends with her now that I'm a Christian. Even though she's been mean to me ever since I've lived with you." Libby sighed unhappily. "Brenda hates me. I guess she always will."

Dad says we should pray for her," said Kevin, his round face serious.

"I guess we should," agreed Libby as she hung her jacket beside Dad's big, red plaid farm coat.

"Hi, kids," greeted Vera with a big smile. "I have hot cocoa and fresh rolls if anyone's interested."

"I can smell them," said Ben excitedly.

"Thanks, Mom."

Vera put her arm around Libby's thin shoulders. "You received a package in the mail today."

"I did?" asked Libby, her hazel eyes wide. "Where from? Who from?" Nobody would send her a package. A cold knot settled in her stomach. Had Mother remembered her birthday? No! Mother wouldn't send her anything. Even when she lived with Mother, she didn't get any presents.

"How big is it?" asked Kevin, brushing his silky blond hair out of his round face, then punching his glasses up.

"About this big," said Vera, measuring with her slender hands. "It's on the table, waiting."

Libby wanted to dash upstairs and not even look at the package, but she followed the others into the dining room. With fumbling fingers she tore off the heavy brown wrapping. Her name was printed in thick, black letters and the address had been marked off twice and new ones put on. The postmark was smudged. It had taken several dollars worth of postage to send it.

"Hurry, Libby," said Susan excitedly. "I want to see what you got."

"Me too," said Kevin, his mouth full of warm bread.

Ice settled around Libby's heart as she saw a white envelope stuck to the gold wrapping under the heavy, brown paper. Her mouth went dry. In bold black letters was written ELIZABETH GAIL DOBBS. With shaking fingers she tore off the envelope. Who was it from? She closed her eyes tight, afraid to look, then slowly opened her eyes. She gasped as she read her father's name at the end of the letter. The letter fluttered from her icy fingers and she plopped down on a chair.

"What is it, Libby?" asked Vera in concern, her arm around Libby. "Don't be frightened. We're all right here with you. You don't have to be scared of anything."

Ben picked up the letter and handed it to his mother.

"It's . . . it's from your father, Frank Dobbs," said Vera hesitantly. "Should I read it to you?"

Libby could only nod yes. How could she get a letter from her father? He was dead. Miss Miller, the social worker, had told her he'd been killed in a car accident a few months ago. Had it been a mistake?

Dear Elizabeth Gail, read Vera. *I know it will be a big surprise for you to get a letter from me, your dad, but I want to get acquainted with you and maybe someday come see you.*

Libby swallowed hard. He couldn't come see her. He was dead. Anyway, she didn't need him. She had a family who loved her. She wasn't just an aid kid now. She belonged to the Johnson family. They couldn't adopt her, but she belonged to them.

Vera continued:

*I left you and your mother because I was a lazy man
without any purpose in life. I didn't want a wife and
baby to hold me down and make me feel guilty for not
making a decent living. I left knowing Marie would*

take care of you. She loved you, Elizabeth Gail. And I didn't. At least, I didn't think I did. But I was wrong. You and your mother were always in my thoughts. Each year on Valentine's Day I would remember your birthday and want to see you. I knew I'd ruin your lives if I did. Your mother and you were probably too happy together to want to see me.

Libby felt bitter tears fill her eyes. She and Mother hadn't been happy.

I'm sending you a box as a twelfth birthday gift. I'm giving the box to a friend along with three letters to send you on dates that I gave him. I was afraid I'd back out and not send anything to you. I'm not very brave, Elizabeth Gail.

By the time you receive the last letter, I may find the courage to come home to you.

The box is a secret box—it holds secrets inside it. I want you to open the box yourself without anyone's help. It will probably take you a long time, but I mean for it to. As you try to open the box I want you to think of me. Try to picture me. Elizabeth Gail, it takes time to know someone and make friends. I want you to learn to love me and forgive me for leaving you. I love you, my daughter. Your father, Frank Dobbs.

Vera wiped her eyes and blew her nose.

Libby blinked away her tears. Did she want to open the box? How could he say he loved her after what he'd done? She didn't need him! She looked at her new family. All of them were there except her new dad, Chuck Johnson. She loved him and he loved her. She didn't need a secret box from a stranger named Frank Dobbs!

"Open the box, Libby," said Vera gently, pushing the

gold-wrapped box in front of Libby.

"No!" cried Libby, pushing her chair back, her eyes wide. "I don't want it! Throw it away!"

"Libby!" said Vera, catching her before she could run away. "Please, honey. Face it. If you throw it away, you'll regret it forever. Your father is dead, so you have nothing to fear from him."

"I don't want to think about *him!*"

"Sit down, Libby," said Vera firmly. "Don't let bitterness or hatred ruin your life. Open the box, then decide what to do."

Libby shrugged. She'd open it, but she wouldn't change her mind. She frowned as she lifted a highly polished wooden box out of the cardboard box.

"It's a Japanese puzzle box," said Ben excitedly. "I've seen one before."

"And it has a secret drawer in it," said Kevin, his eyes round.

Libby shoved the box toward Ben. "Open it for me. We might as well see the secret inside." She sounded bitter, her voice sharp.

Ben laughed uncertainly. "I can't open it, Libby. I don't know how."

"Besides, your dad wants you to do it by yourself," said Susan, picking up the heavy box and turning it over and over. "You can't even see how it could open!"

"Let me look," said Kevin, taking it from Susan. "A mystery box, Libby. I wonder what's inside?"

"I don't know and I don't care!" said Libby. She wouldn't try to open it. She wouldn't think about her dad. She'd hide the box away and leave it hidden forever!

TWO
The trouble box

Libby flung the polished box onto her bed. She didn't want to look at it or touch it. How could that man dare think she wanted to know him! She hated him! How could he leave her when she was three years old, then expect her to forgive and love him?

Libby yanked off her school clothes and jerked on blue jeans and a faded orange sweatshirt.

The bedroom door burst open and Susan rushed in. She had on blue jeans and a light blue sweatshirt. Her red-gold hair was in two pony tails, one at each ear, that flipped constantly as Susan moved. "Oh, Libby!" cried Susan excitedly. "Let me try to open your box. I want to know what's inside. Don't you?" She reached for the box, but Libby pushed her away.

"Don't touch it," screamed Libby, her fists knotted at her sides, her feet apart. "I don't want anybody around it."

"But, Libby! Not even me? We're sisters," whispered Susan, almost in tears.

"Not real sisters," snapped Libby, her pointed chin high in the air.

Tears filled Susan's blue eyes. "I know not real ones, but I thought we were learning to love each other like real sisters."

Libby wanted to throw her arms around Susan and tell her she was sorry, but she was too upset about the polished box lying on her multicolored bedspread. "I don't want you around my box, Susan. You can't touch it. You can't look at it." She stepped close to Susan. "If you come in my room when I'm not here to try to open it, you'll be sorry!"

"You think you're so big!" cried Susan, her hands on her hips, her eyes blazing. "I don't care about you and your old box. And I wish your real dad was alive so you could go live with him!" Susan dashed from the room, slamming the door behind her.

Libby dropped to her bed, her face white. Did Susan really wish that? Libby reached for Pinky, the big pink stuffed dog that Susan had given her as a welcoming gift when she first came. Libby always hugged Pinky when she was upset or happy or excited.

The sight of the highly polished wooden box made her furious. She leaped up, grabbed the box, and flung it into the red wastebasket beside her desk. The basket rocked, then tipped, spilling the box, wadded paper, and a gum wrapper onto the pink carpet. Tears stung Libby's eyes. She didn't want the box. She didn't want to read letters from her real dad. She wanted to be happy with the Johnson family here on their farm. She wanted to continue enjoying her red and dark pink room, the most beautiful room she'd ever seen in her twelve years. She wanted Ben and Kevin Johnson as brothers. She wanted Susan Johnson as her sister, and Chuck and Vera Johnson as her dad and mom.

A distant call from Vera, telling them all to do their chores, sent Libby scurrying. She picked up the fallen basket and papers, then plunked the box on her desk and stuffed the letter in her drawer. She had to get at the chores. One of the rules was doing all outdoor chores before supper. At her other foster homes in the city, she'd only had indoor chores. Here she had both to do.

She flew down the carpeted stairs and to the back porch. Ben was just going out. Susan and Kevin were pulling on their boots. Susan wouldn't look at Libby. By the time Libby had her work jacket on, Susan was outdoors, letting in a blast of cold air before she slammed the door.

"Did you try to open your box?" asked Kevin as he tugged on his thick mittens.

"No!" snapped Libby, pulling on her boots. "And don't ask me about it again." Why couldn't she stay calm and answer politely?

"I'm going to tell on you," cried Kevin, his round face red with anger. "Dad told you not to talk mean anymore."

"I can talk as mean as I want," screamed Libby as she jerked the door open, then slammed it behind her. The cold air felt good against her hot face. Why didn't everyone leave her alone? She rushed toward the sheep pasture, tears stinging her eyes. Goosy Poosy honked, but didn't follow her.

In a daze Libby fed and watered the sheep. How fat they looked in their winter wool.

Libby walked toward the horse barn, glad when Rex joined her. He barked playfully until she stroked him. Then he walked sedately beside her, her hand resting lightly on his head. The big collie made her feel better.

Would Ben expect her to go riding with him today? Or would he realize she was too upset? Riding Star or Apache Girl usually made her feel terrific, but not now.

She opened the barn door, then led each horse from the pen into his stall. She fed them, not taking time to talk to them and pet them as she usually did.

At Snowball's stall she walked in just to be with the little filly. Snowball belonged to her. The family had given her Snowball for a birthday present. Libby smiled, tears pricking her eyelids. How surprised and happy she'd been. "Oh, Snowball!" she whispered huskily as she hugged the filly. Tears slid down her cheeks. She loved Snowball. She loved her foster family. They loved her. How could she have talked so mean to them? When would she learn to be good? "Jesus," she whispered, her face against Snowball's neck. "Forgive me for being bad. Help me to watch how I act and what I say. I do love you and I love my new family."

With a shaky smile, Libby walked out of the barn. She blinked against the sparkling bright snow. She looked around at the many farm buildings, then up at the house. She thought of the first day she'd seen it. It had been a house with a capital H, a really wonderful, beautiful house. And now it was her home!

Just then Susan came from feeding the yearling steers. She stopped when she saw Libby.

Libby walked to her. "I'm sorry, Susan," said Libby, smiling warmly. "You can look at my box anytime you want. You can even open it if you want."

Susan smiled too. "I won't try, Libby. Your dad wanted you to open it alone. And I didn't really mean it when I said I wished you lived with him. I'm glad you live here with us."

Libby wanted to do a handspring right in the snow. "Do you need help with your math tonight?"

"No." She beamed with pleasure. "I passed that test today that you helped me study for last night."

"That's great! I guess I'd better finish my chores so I can practice my piano." Libby dashed toward the cow barn. She had a special calf that had to have salve on its leg. She always offered to take care of the sick or hurt animals. She liked to make them feel better. Dad told her she had a special touch for animals. Libby smiled happily, pushing the thoughts of her box to the back of her mind.

Ben was hooking up the milkers to the eight milk cows as she walked in. A barn cat rubbed against her leg.

"Did you see Chester?" asked Libby. That was the name she'd given the calf.

"I just looked in," answered Ben, looking up with a smile. "He's better. Dad will be glad to hear that. He thought he might have to call the vet."

Libby took the can of salve to the next-to-the-last stall. "Hi, Chester," she said, rubbing her hand down his side to his leg. The sore was better. She dabbed salve on it, talking softly to him. She wrinkled her nose at the smell of the salve. How could such a bad-smelling thing do any good?

She walked back down the aisle to stand beside Ben. He looked good even with his old barn coat and dirty boots on. She smiled. "I didn't try to open my box," she said softly. "I think I'll put it away and leave it. Maybe when I grow up I'll be able to open it."

"Do you hate your real dad?" asked Ben in surprise.

"Yes," she admitted reluctantly. She didn't want Ben thinking bad of her.

"You know what Dad says about hating anyone," said Ben, stooping down to pick up a black barn cat.

"I know," she said stiffly. She didn't want to think about hating or not hating. Suddenly she wanted to do something vigorous. "Did you get the stall cleaned?"

"Not yet," said Ben.

"I'll do it," she said, rushing to find a pitchfork, then hurrying to the stall that Dad had said needed to be cleaned today for sure. She worked hard at it so she wouldn't think of anything else. By the time she finished she felt better, but tired. Ben was unhooking the milkers as she left the barn.

Libby hurried to the house, anxious to practice the piano. She loved touching the keys. Someday she wanted to play the piano at a concert featuring only herself. Should she advertise using Elizabeth Gail Dobbs? Or maybe by then the Johnsons could adopt her, and she would be Elizabeth Gail Johnson.

THREE
Brenda

Libby slipped her long, yellow-flowered nightgown over her head, then wriggled it into place. She brushed her short, brown hair, then dropped the brush on her dresser. She yawned. Was it still snowing out? Maybe they'd have a snow day tomorrow and school would be closed. She and Susan could play Ping-Pong in the basement. Or maybe they could play Monopoly.

The lamp on her desk glowed brightly, showing off the Japanese puzzle box's shiny surface. Libby didn't want to look at it or think about it. She had tried hard not to think about it. Slowly she picked it up, turning it over and over. It was smooth on every side. How could she possibly open it? What was inside? She clamped her thin lips tightly. She didn't want to know what was inside.

A light tap at the door startled her. Hastily she set the box down and called, "Come in," her back to the box. She smiled in delight as Chuck came in, his red hair slightly mussed, his hazel eyes twinkling.

"I thought you'd be in bed, fast asleep," he said, smiling.

"I was almost ready to climb in bed, Dad," she said grinning.

He walked to the desk and picked up the box, turning it over. "I want to talk to you, anyway," he said gently.

Libby wanted to grab the box and toss it away. She didn't need another dad or gifts from another dad. Her heart raced.

"Elizabeth," he said. She smiled, loving to hear him say her name. He was the only person that called her Elizabeth. "Mom told me about this box from your father," continued Chuck softly. "She told me what was in the letter and how upset you were."

"I didn't want to hear from him," she said stiffly, her hands locked behind her back.

Chuck sat down on the desk chair, the box still in his hands. Libby sank down on the edge of her bed, picking up Pinky and hugging him close. He felt soft and warm and comforting.

"In the three and a half months you've lived with us, we've all learned to love you very much, Elizabeth, and you love us. You've also learned to love Jesus!" Chuck looked down at the box, then across to Libby. "This is a step of growing. Face what comes your way."

Libby squirmed uneasily.

"Your father is dead, so he can't be hurt by your hate and bitterness. But you will be, Elizabeth, if you don't get rid of those feelings. Can't you do as your father asked?"

Libby's stomach tightened. She couldn't! "Do I have to?" she asked fiercely.

"It's for your own good."

"Can't I just put the box away and forget about it?" she whispered hoarsely.

"It wouldn't work that way, would it, honey?" Chuck pushed his red hair off his wide forehead. "The longer you put it off, the harder it will be on you. Ask Jesus to take away your hate and bitterness and fill you with his love."

Libby carefully laid Pinky on her pillow, then stood up, tears in her eyes. "I will ask Jesus to take away my bad feelings," she said. "But please, don't make me try to open the box. I don't want to think about my real dad."

Chuck put his arms around her and kissed her. "Put the box away if you must for a while. We'll be praying that God gives you the strength and courage to face it. You're happy with us and we're happy with you. Thinking of your father won't change any of that."

"How do you know?" she cried. "Maybe it's only a trick to get me back. Maybe he's not really dead and he'll make me go live with him."

"Hey, honey," he said, holding her close. "We know that isn't possible. Miss Miller wouldn't have told you if it hadn't been true. Don't cry. You're here to stay!"

Finally she dried her eyes and blew her nose. How awful to cry in front of Dad! He really must think she was a baby.

"I guess you'd better get to bed," he said. "That school bus comes very early in the morning. Good night, Elizabeth."

" 'Night, Dad," she whispered, kissing him again. She closed the door after him, then turned to stare at the box. She didn't need two dads. Chuck was all she needed. She'd try not to hate her real dad, but she would not open the box or think about him.

Libby grabbed the box, opened her closet, and stuffed it back in a dark corner on the top shelf. There! That's where it was going to stay forever!

She knelt beside her bed to pray, remembering to ask Jesus to take away her bad feelings. She did feel a little better. As long as she forced her thoughts away from her real dad, she was all right.

She slept poorly. The next day she walked through the school halls tiredly. It had been so hard to wake up. Susan had had to call her twice, then finally shake her hard to wake her.

Libby stuffed her math book into her locker, then clicked it shut.

"Hey, Libby!"

She looked up, then smiled as Joe Wilkens hurried to her side. She liked the red shirt he was wearing. His brown hair hung almost to his dark eyebrows. His eyes were so brown that they looked black at times. She knew he liked her a lot. She liked him, too.

"Ben told me about that box you got in the mail," said Joe as they walked through the noisy, crowded hall toward the cafeteria. "Did you open it yet?"

"No," she said sharply, wishing Ben would have kept his big mouth shut. Ben should have realized she didn't want it known. "I put it away and I don't want to open it."

"I will!" said Joe excitedly. "It shouldn't take me long."

"Nobody's going to," she said impatiently.

"Oh," he said in disappointment just as his sister Brenda joined them.

Libby nodded hello, but didn't say anything. Brenda was always so mean to her that she didn't want to start anything.

"I didn't know you had a dad," said Brenda, bumping Libby with her tray.

Oh, that Ben! Why hadn't he kept his big mouth shut? Libby bit her bottom lip to keep from saying something terrible to Brenda.

"Aid kids do have dads," continued Brenda, loud enough so that others around would be sure to hear. "It's just that aid kids aren't wanted by their dads or mothers."

"Shut up, Brenda," said Joe, grabbing his sister's arm tightly.

Libby's heart raced with anger and humiliation. She wanted to jerk out Brenda's long, black hair.

"You might like aid kids, Joe, but I don't," snapped Brenda, jerking away from Joe.

Libby knotted her fists, thinking of the time she'd socked Brenda and given her a bloody nose. How she wished she could do it again!

"Did your dad send you a fortune in that secret box?" asked Brenda maliciously. "Maybe you'll have enough money so you can leave the Johnsons, and they won't have to put up with you any longer."

Libby moved to fly at her, but Joe caught her arm.

"You'll get in trouble," he whispered insistently. "Get away, Brenda."

Libby felt as if a million eyes were staring at her. Oh, how she wanted to hit Brenda! But she couldn't. It would hurt Chuck and Vera too much.

"Are you scared of me, aid kid?" asked Brenda smugly.

24

Libby felt hot, then cold. "I am not afraid of you, Brenda Wilkens. I could beat you up with both hands tied behind my back. If you want another bloody nose from me, then I'll be glad to give you one."

Brenda quickly stepped back. The kids giggled, whispering noisily.

Libby stepped closer to Brenda. "I don't want to hear anymore about my box! And I don't want to be called 'aid kid'!"

Brenda scurried behind one of the eighth-grade boys, then peeked around him. "I hope your box is full of poison, aid kid!" she screamed.

"I'm telling Mom on you, Brenda," said Joe angrily. "You know what she'll do after all that trouble you caused Libby already."

Libby locked her fingers together, forcing the anger away as Brenda hurried to cut in line farther ahead.

"You OK, Libby?" asked Joe softly.

"Sure," she said, smiling. "Thanks, Joe." She was glad she hadn't beat Brenda up. She smelled the fried chicken. Suddenly she was very, very hungry.

FOUR
Toby Smart

Three days went by without anyone asking Libby
about her box. She hadn't looked at it, and she tried
not to think about it.

Libby closed her book and looked at the others in the
family room. Vera was at the piano, playing the song
that she was to play in church Sunday. Susan was
studying math. Ben and Kevin were playing chess.
Ben always beat Kevin. Libby sighed as she looked at
the mantle clock. It was already time for Miss Miller
to bring Toby Smart.

Libby opened her book and tried again to read.
Would Toby Smart be happy with the Johnson family?
Had he ever lived in the country before? Would he like
her the best since they were both aid kids?

The sound of a car in the drive sent Libby flying to
the window. She pressed her face against it. Yes, it was
Miss Miller in the same car that she had used to bring
her out in November.

"Are they here? Are they here?" asked Kevin, crowd-
ing Libby away from the window.

"Kevin! Libby! Away from the window, please," commanded Vera as she hurried to the front door. She pushed her blonde hair away from her face and tugged her red sweater down over her red plaid slacks. "You did pen up Goosy Poosy, didn't you, Ben?"

"Yes," he said, craning his neck to see out the window without pressing against it. Libby thought he looked great in his blue pullover and jeans.

"Oh, Libby!" exclaimed Susan, grabbing her arm and jumping up and down. "This is as exciting as the day you first came." Susan's red-gold hair bobbed up and down. Her blue eyes were wide.

"Is he really sucking his thumb?" asked Kevin in disgust as he leaned closer to the window. "What a baby. I thought he was almost my age."

Vera turned to them, her face sober. "You are not to tease him about sucking his thumb. Understand? Once he feels secure and loved, he'll stop."

Libby smiled, glad to hear Vera's words. She knew how terrible it was to be teased. She waited breathlessly as Vera opened the door. Cold air blasted in.

Miss Miller smiled warmly at Libby, then looked down at the redheaded, freckle-faced boy beside her. "This is Toby Smart," she said brightly.

Libby watched as Vera greeted Toby, then introduced him to each of them. Libby smiled her friendliest smile, but Toby looked scared. Why, he seemed more afraid of her than the others. She frowned, feeling disappointed. Why should he be scared of her?

Miss Miller walked to Libby, sliding her arm around Libby's thin shoulders. Libby smelled the beautiful aroma of her perfume. "How are you, Libby?" she asked in a soft voice.

"OK," answered Libby, smiling. Miss Miller looked so pretty today. Her brown hair was parted on the side and hung to her shoulders. Long dark lashes surrounded her bright blue eyes.

"Toby will be fine before long," said Miss Miller, only for Libby's ears. "Give him time. He's a very quiet, scared boy. Because he's so big for his age, he has a hard time getting along with other kids."

Libby studied Toby. She knew he was eight years old, but he was as tall as ten-year-old Kevin. He wasn't quite as roly poly as Kevin. She watched as Toby tried to hide behind Vera, his thumb in his mouth.

"We'll show you your room," said Kevin and Ben together.

Toby hung back, his thumb tight in his mouth, his hazel eyes bright with unshed tears.

Poor Toby Smart. Libby wanted to hug him and tell him everything would be all right. She stepped toward him, then stopped, seeing the look of terror on his face. He really was more afraid of her than anyone! She turned to ask Miss Miller about it, then stopped. Miss Miller would only say she was imagining things.

"Go ahead with the boys, Toby," said Vera gently. "You'll find some nice surprises there just for you. We're so glad you've come to live with us."

Libby watched as they walked up the wide carpeted stairs. Would Toby like the giant teddy bear she'd bought him? He was sure to like the truck and cement mixer the others bought.

"Will you stay for a cup of coffee, Miss Miller?" asked Vera with a smile.

Miss Miller looked at her watch, then sighed. "I'd love to, but I really must rush." She turned to Libby.

"Did you get that big box that I forwarded to you?"

Libby's face turned pale. She swallowed hard as she nodded.

"I'm glad you did, even though it was a few days late for your birthday," said Miss Miller. She waited expectantly, but Libby couldn't say a word. "I'll see you in two weeks, Mrs. Johnson. 'Bye, girls." The cold air rushed in as she opened the door. "Oh, dear. It's snowing again. I will be glad when winter's over."

"We will, too," said Vera. "Drive carefully." She closed the door, then smiled at the girls. "We have a new person in our family."

"Let's show him the horses," said Susan, grabbing Libby's arm and tugging her toward the stairs.

"I hope he likes horses," said Libby.

As they walked into Toby's blue room, Libby saw Toby sitting quietly on the edge of the bed. The boys were talking fast and showing him everything around the room. Toby didn't seem at all impressed with the room or with his new family. When he saw Libby he scooted to the back of the bed, his face suddenly very white.

"We came to show Toby the horses," said Susan, smiling at Toby.

Libby felt like crying. Why was he so afraid of her? He even held out his hand for Susan when she reached out hers and asked him if he wanted to go to the barn to see the horses. "I'll take your other hand," said Libby, forcing a smile.

Toby hid his hand behind him and moved closer to Susan. Libby looked up quickly at Ben to see if he'd noticed Toby's actions. Ben hadn't. Should she tell Ben?

Libby shrugged, then followed them downstairs.

Maybe Toby didn't like her looks. Susan was small and dainty and very pretty. Libby was tall and thin with ordinary brown hair, hazel eyes, and a pointed chin.

She listened to the others chattering to Toby as they all put on their coats and boots. He didn't answer any of them, but he didn't seem afraid of them. Once he even smiled at Susan. Libby followed them to the barn. Rex ran to her side and waited for her to pet him. At least *he* liked her best. She hugged him, blinking back her tears.

Goosy Poosy honked loudly and indignantly.

"That's our pet goose," said Kevin. "He doesn't like to be shut up in the chicken pen. He thinks he's better than the hens."

"He *is* better," said Susan. "We don't have any hens that will ride down the hill on our sled!"

"You should see Goosy Poosy on Kevin's sled," said Ben, laughing, then describing the goose and Kevin sliding together.

Libby laughed, then stopped as Toby actually laughed, too. What could *she* say to make him laugh? If she could make him laugh, maybe he'd learn he didn't have to be afraid of her.

They walked through the barn, Ben and Susan taking turns telling Toby about each horse. Kevin offered to let him ride his pony Sleepy if he wanted to, but Toby shook his head no.

"Here are Jack and Dan," said Ben proudly as they stopped by the big, gray draft horses. Jack lifted his hoof and shook his head. Toby jumped back.

Libby smiled. She remembered how she'd felt the first time she'd seen the horses. She hadn't been afraid at all. Learning to ride had been a dream come true.

30

Maybe she could teach Toby to ride. A yellow barn cat rubbed against her leg. She picked him up and cradled him in her arms. The cat purred contentedly. Libby rubbed her cheek against his soft fur. He smelled like hay and old milk.

"Here's Libby's filly," said Susan, pointing to Snowball. "We gave Snowball to Libby on her birthday, February 14."

"Libby's our Valentine sweetheart," said Kevin, grinning up at Libby. "I like to tease her about it."

"And get in trouble for it," said Libby, grinning too.

"When's your birthday, Toby?" asked Ben, leaning against the stall and looking at the younger boy.

Libby didn't think he was going to answer, but finally he said in a voice barely above a whisper, "March 2nd."

"Hey that's only a few days away," said Susan happily. "We'll have a birthday party for you, Toby."

"What would you like for a present?" asked Libby excitedly.

Toby hid behind Susan and wouldn't answer.

Libby tried to hide her hurt feelings. Toby *was* afraid of her. But why?

FIVE
The skating party

Libby stood unsteadily on her ice skates. She wanted to skim across the pond dressed in a short, red skating dress like she'd seen on one of the Olympic skaters on television. Would she ever learn to skate as well as the others? Even Kevin could make figure eights and circles.

"Don't be scared, Elizabeth," said Chuck, skating up beside her, with Toby on his arm.

"I'm not scared," said Libby breathlessly as she clutched Chuck's other arm to keep from falling. She didn't look at Toby. She knew he'd hide his face against Dad's arm if she did.

"Just do what we showed you before," said Chuck, smiling reassuringly at her. He had on a black snowmobile suit trimmed with white. Toby was dressed in a red, white, and blue snowmobile suit that Mom had bought specially for tonight's skating party.

"I'll try," said Libby, carefully turning loose of Chuck. Slowly she slid along the smooth ice as Chuck and Toby glided away. Maybe she should have stayed in the house. With all the kids from their Sunday school class there, the pond seemed suddenly very crowded. It would be so embarrassing to fall. She quickly looked at Brenda, knowing how *she* would laugh to see Libby fall.

"You're doing just fine, Libby," called Connie Tol as she and her husband Ron skated past. Connie was Libby's Sunday school teacher.

Libby smiled. She liked Connie. The Bible stories she told were always interesting and exciting.

"Want to skate with me, Libby?" asked Susan, skating up beside Libby.

"Don't go fast," begged Libby as she crossed her arms to hang on as Susan had taught her. "It is easier this way."

"Did you notice Brenda just had to come tonight?" whispered Susan, making a face.

"Yeah," said Libby, wrinkling her nose. "She has to spoil everything. Watch her show off. She thinks she's so big."

"She does skate well," Susan had to admit. "She thinks someday she'll skate in the Olympics!" Susan's nose was red from the cold. Her blue eyes sparkled excitedly. "*I* would like to skate in the Olympics, myself."

"*I* would just like to skate well enough to keep from falling," said Libby with a laugh. "Toby's not doing too bad, is he?"

"Not for his first time on skates," said Susan as they watched Toby skating back and forth between Chuck and Ben.

"Susan, why doesn't Toby like me?" asked Libby sadly.

Susan looked up at her in surprise. "How do you know he doesn't like you?"

"By the way he acts," answered Libby sharply. "You must have noticed."

Susan shrugged. "He's just shy, I guess."

But Libby knew it was more than that. "Is it because I'm not cute like you?"

Susan laughed. "Oh, Libby. You're being funny."

Libby didn't say any more about it. She forced her thoughts off Toby. It was great skating with Susan!

Smoke from the bonfire drifted across the pond. Floodlights around the pond lighted the area, leaving the surrounding farmyard in shadows.

"Here comes Joe," whispered Susan excitedly. "I think he wants to skate with you."

Libby felt her face grow redder as Joe stopped beside them. Would he really want to skate with her? "Hi, Joe," she said breathlessly.

"Hi, Joe," said Susan, grinning from one to the other.

Libby wanted to push her down for teasing. Too bad David Boomer hadn't come or she could have teased Susan about him.

"Want to skate with me, Libby?" asked Joe. His cheeks were red from the cold.

"Sure," said Libby, holding her hands out to him.

"Could I ask you something?" asked Joe hesitantly.

"What?"

"Promise you won't get mad."

Libby laughed. What could make her mad at him? "Ask me."

"Did you open your box yet?" asked Joe eagerly.

"No!" she exclaimed impatiently. Why did he have to remind her of that?

"You said you wouldn't get mad."

"I'm not going to open that box!"

"OK. OK."

They skated in silence. Libby had tried so hard to forget the box. She really wasn't angry, but she wished Joe would forget about the box, too.

"Your new brother is really learning to skate, isn't he?" asked Joe.

Libby was glad he had stopped talking about the box. "He sure is having fun." She laughed as Toby flapped his arms wildly for balance. Suddenly he plopped down on the ice, a surprised look on his face.

Joe laughed.

"It's not funny!" cried Libby, pulling free from Joe. "I'm going to help him."

"You don't need to," said Joe, skating beside her. "Brenda's going to."

Brenda! Would Toby allow Brenda to help him? Libby reached his side just as Brenda did.

"Here, Toby," Libby said, reaching from him.

Toby scooted away from her, his hazel eyes wide with fright.

Brenda laughed. "You're a smart kid, Toby. I don't like her either."

Libby's face burned. She bit her lip to keep from saying something mean to Brenda.

"Come on, Toby. I'll help you," said Brenda, lifting Toby to his feet. She looked triumphantly at Libby. "He likes *me.*"

"Don't start anything, Brenda," said Joe fiercely, frowning.

"I'm not," said Brenda, making a face. She started away with Toby, then looked over her shoulder at Libby. "Did you find the secret in your mystery box, aid kid?"

Libby's heart raced with anger. She knotted her fists as she started after Brenda. Suddenly her feet flew out from under her, and she landed hard on her back. How embarrassing! She wanted to die.

"Are you all right?" asked Joe anxiously as he helped her up.

"No," she snapped, pulling away from him. She

wanted to hide in her room and never face any of them again. Just how many of the kids had seen her fall? It was all that Brenda's fault!

"Are you hurt, Libby?" asked Connie, stopping beside Joe and Libby.

"No," mumbled Libby, her face bright red. Suddenly her green snowmobile suit felt too hot and tight.

"This is a wonderful night for a skating party," said Connie, taking Libby's arm and skating slowly across the ice behind Jean and Pete Laurence. "All the kids are having a great time. You have a very special family, Libby. I know you're proud of them."

Libby glowed with pleasure.

"I want to thank you for helping with the party tonight. Vera told me that each of you worked hard getting everything ready for us."

"It was fun," said Libby, smiling.

A long blast from a whistle cut through the air.

"Your mother is calling us in for hot dogs," said Connie. "I'm starved, aren't you?"

"Yes," said Libby, surprised that she was. She could hardly wait to take off her skates and roast a hot dog over the fire.

With fumbling fingers, Libby removed her skates and slipped on her snow boots. How good it felt to be on solid, firm ground again.

Shouts and laughter filled the air. Libby wanted to push in line and be one of the first to grab a hot dog, but Mom had told them that guests were always first.

"Are you hungry?" asked Ben, stopping beside her.

"I sure am!" she exclaimed. The bonfire was large enough for several to stand around it at a time. "I'd like to be eating right now."

"Me, too," said Ben, grinning. "I guess I could eat ten hot dogs."

"I'd leave room for marshmallows," said Libby, her mouth watering.

By the time she got to the bonfire with her hot dog, she felt hungry enough to eat ten hot dogs. The fire felt warm against her face as she squatted near it, holding her hot dog over the glowing embers. Toby was just across from her. She could see he had already scraped his hot dog in the ashes and that it was burned on one side. She smiled secretly as she thought of what she could do for Toby. She'd fix her hot dog just right and give it to him. That should make him feel good. Maybe then he'd know she really wanted to be friends with him.

Libby heard several of the kids talking about the sledding party they were having the following week at Marvin Jones' house. Brenda asked if she could come. They said she could, and Libby sighed. Someday she'd have a party and tell Brenda that she wasn't invited. Libby sighed again. No, she couldn't do that.

Finally the hot dog was done. Libby carried it to the table. She picked up a paper plate and a bun. She could see Toby screwing up his face as he bit into his hot dog. She put everything on the hot dog, then dropped a handful of potato chips on the plate. Toby would be so pleased. Libby smiled as she picked up a cup of hot cocoa with a partly melted marshmallow swimming in it. She carried the plate and the cup to Toby. "I made this for you, Toby," she said, smiling as she held them out to him.

He popped his thumb in his mouth and backed away.

"I see you made a friend," said Brenda, laughing at Libby.

"Here, Toby," said Libby impatiently. "It's yours."

Toby ran to Brenda and hid his face against her arm.

Brenda laughed harder as she looked from Libby to Toby.

Libby plunked the plate and cup on the table, her face red, a hard knot in her stomach. She walked away from the table, away from all the kids who were having so much fun. She wasn't hungry anymore.

SIX
A letter for Libby

For the third time, Libby played "The Song from Down Under" on the piano. It had a pretty sound, but Libby didn't like it. It made her think of Mother. She knew her mother was in Australia. But for how long? Would she come back this year and demand to take Libby home?

Libby covered her fluttering heart. What if Mother came back and signed the release papers that would give the Johnsons permission to adopt her? That would be the most wonderful thing that could happen to her! She smiled dreamily as she lovingly touched the ivory piano keys to play the song again. But what if they really didn't want to adopt her? She gasped, her fingers suddenly icy and clumsy. They liked her well enough as a foster daughter, but maybe she wasn't good enough to be an *adopted* daughter.

Her own dad hadn't wanted her. He'd left her when she was three years old. If your own dad can't stand to be with you, something really is wrong. Was it her looks? Or maybe she was the type of person that nobody could love. Toby couldn't stand the sight of her.

Hot tears stung Libby's eyes. She blinked hard as

she turned the page to try another song. Awkwardly she fumbled through it.

"Go slower and concentrate," said Vera, coming to stand behind Libby. "You are a natural at the piano."

Libby's chin dropped to her chest. Vera's hands smelled of onions. "Why . . . why doesn't Toby like me?" asked Libby in a tight voice.

Vera kissed the top of Libby's head, then leaned her cheek against it. "I can't understand his attitude, Libby, I really can't. Chuck and I were discussing it just last night after the skating party. We both noticed how he acted. He really is afraid of you." Vera walked around and sat beside Libby on the piano bench. "Have you given him any reason to be afraid of you?"

Libby shook her head no, biting her bottom lip in agitation. She looked at Vera in agony. "Am I ugly, Mom?"

Vera slid her arm around Libby's waist. "Of course not!" She frowned thoughtfully. "I don't think Toby would be afraid just because of your looks. It has to be something else. Dad tried to talk to him about you, but Toby wouldn't talk."

Libby blinked back her tears. She would not cry! "What can I do, Mom? It makes me feel so bad!"

Vera took Libby's hand in hers. "We've told you the answer to any problem is with God. We'll pray about it and ask God to give all of us wisdom on how to act with Toby. God knows Toby and God knows us. He'll help us find the answer."

Libby looked into Vera's pretty blue eyes. "Did you pray for wisdom for me?"

Vera smiled, then kissed the tip of Libby's nose. "We sure did. And God answered."

Libby smiled, feeling warm all over. Mom did love her. She loved Mom. If Mom said God would take care of the problem with Toby, then he would take care of it.

"Libby! Libby!" cried Kevin, bursting into the room, his coat still on. "The mailman just brought you another letter! Another letter from your real dad!" Kevin's round face beamed with pleasure. His cheeks and nose were red from cold. Snow clung to his coat.

Libby's heart sank. She licked her dry lips as she stumbled away from the piano bench. She didn't want the letter. She wanted to run upstairs and hide in her room.

"Take it, Libby," said Vera softly as she held out the letter. "Read it. It's better to face our difficulties than to put them behind us."

Reluctantly, Libby took the letter. Her face was pale. Her hands shook so hard she couldn't tear open the envelope.

"Shall I?" asked Vera.

Libby shoved the letter into Vera's hand, nodding hard and trying to keep the tears from falling. Why did a letter have to come today and spoil everything?

"Hurry, Mom," cried Kevin, bouncing around excitedly.

"Shall I read it aloud?" asked Vera as she pulled the letter out.

Libby nodded again, her heart racing. She didn't want to know what it said. She wanted to pitch it into the crackling fire and watch it disappear.

Vera pulled her down beside her on the couch. "Do you want Kevin to leave the room?"

Libby shook her head no, then shrugged. What did it matter?

Dear Elizabeth Gail, read Vera, smiling reassuringly at Libby. *Have you opened the box yet?*

Libby cringed, thinking of the box hidden in the dark corner of her closet.

Vera continued reading.

I think it will be a while before you figure out how to open it. You must slide the right combination of wood pieces before it will open to reveal the secret drawer.

I bet you are a big girl now, and very pretty. I wonder if you look like me or like your mother.

Libby's stomach knotted. Mother wouldn't like it at all if she talked about Dad, even if Mother were around to talk.

I want to tell you something about myself, Elizabeth Gail. I've been working on a small ranch in Nebraska for four years. Before that I drifted from place to place, from job to job. When I saw the sandhills of western Nebraska, I decided I wanted to spend some time there. There's just me and Old Zeb. He owns the ranch. His parents came to Nebraska and claimed this ranch during the Homestead Act. Have you studied about that in school?

Libby frowned, not caring if she'd studied about it or not.

Old Zeb put me right to work even though I am blind in one eye.

Libby gasped. Blind in one eye! How awful!

I can ride a horse. You would have laughed if you'd seen your old dad learn to ride. I help fix fences, round up cattle, hay, and cook for myself and Old Zeb. He still does things the old-fashioned way. He likes it better that way. So do I. He doesn't even own a car. I finally persuaded him to ride to town in mine one day, but he wouldn't do it again. He drives his team of horses and his wagon to town about once a month. He says that's all a fellow needs of that crazy town life.

Nobody would know me dressed in my cowboy boots and jeans and western shirt. My hat is an old one of Zeb's that he thought was too fancy. But, I like it.

I don't get paid much, but I get all I can eat and a place to sleep and call home. Maybe Old Zeb will let me bring you here for a visit. Would you like that, Elizabeth Gail?

Libby clenched her hands together, not wanting to feel the excitement she felt. A real ranch, lots of horses, and her dad with one blind eye.

Kevin squirmed excitedly.

Keep trying to open your box, daughter. And think about me often. With all my love, your dad, Frank Dobbs.

Vera laid the letter on Libby's lap, wiping tears from her eyes. "Oh, Libby, he is only asking a little of you. For your own good, forget how he deserted you. Think how much he loved you and wanted you."

Libby blinked hard to keep the tears back. She didn't want them to know how she felt right now.

"Old Zeb sounds great," said Kevin. "And your dad was a cowboy, Libby. That's super!"

Libby pushed herself up. "I'll put the letter with the other one," she said huskily. She dashed to the hall and up the stairs to her room.

She opened the drawer where she'd stuffed the first letter, then shoved the new one in. "With all my love, your dad, Frank Dobbs." Love! Tears filled her eyes and ran down her pale cheeks. She flung herself onto her bed and cried against Pinky.

"Libby!" called Susan. "Libby, come here."

Libby pushed herself up. Her head ached. Her throat felt swollen.

"Libby!" called Susan, louder this time.

Quickly Libby blew her nose, then wiped her eyes. What could Susan want? Whatever it was, she hoped it would keep her mind off Frank Dobbs. She was done, really done thinking about him.

Susan was waiting in the kitchen for Libby. Susan wiped the milk off her mouth, then bit into a fresh cinnamon roll.

"What do you want?" asked Libby, resting her hands on the back of the kitchen chair.

Susan swallowed, then smiled. "Guess who's here?"

For one wild, scary moment Libby thought of her real dad, then she knew it couldn't be. "Who?" she asked, her mouth dry.

"Mom took them to the guest room. They're staying until tomorrow afternoon."

"Who?" asked Libby sharply. She didn't like Susan teasing her like this.

Susan brushed crumbs off her pink flowered blouse, a smug look on her pretty face. "Grandma and Grandpa," she said, her blue eyes sparkling happily.

Libby's heart leaped with joy. She smiled. It had been a long time since they'd been to visit. Suddenly the smile vanished. What if they wouldn't like her anymore? They might decide they didn't want her in their family. Maybe they'd talk to Chuck and Vera and convince them to send her to another home.

"What's wrong with you, Libby?" asked Susan impatiently. "You look so funny."

"Oh, leave me alone!" snapped Libby, locking her

fingers together. "I'm going outdoors."

"Now?" asked Susan in surprise leaping up and hurrying to Libby's side. "But you haven't even said hello to Grandma and Grandpa."

Libby turned and headed for the back porch to get her outdoor clothes. It would be better to stay away from Grandma and Grandpa. Then she'd never have to know if they didn't want her.

"Here you are, Libby," said Vera, catching Libby's arm. "Look who's here to visit." She smiled from Libby to the gray-haired couple beside her.

Libby stiffened.

"How are you, Libby?" asked Grandma, smiling.

Libby finally managed to say "Fine."

"We brought you a birthday gift," said Grandpa in his deep voice. He rubbed his hand over his hair. "Do you think you could stand a gift even though it's late?" His blue eyes twinkled.

Libby relaxed enough to smile warmly. Maybe they did still like her.

"Come into the family room, Libby," said Grandma, taking Libby's arm. "We'll let you have it now."

"What is it?" asked Susan excitedly. "I want to see."

"You mean *you* want to open it," teased Grandpa, ruffling Susan's hair.

Susan laughed. "If Libby doesn't hurry up, I will open it."

Libby wanted to stay beside Grandma. She felt soft and smelled good. Slowly Libby lifted the large package. It was tied with a bright red bow. It would be terrible to tear the red and white paper.

"Hurry, Libby," said Vera, laughing. "I can't wait either."

Libby wished this good feeling would last forever. She carefully took off the paper as the others chattered back and forth. Soft music from the stereo drifted through the room.

What could it be? Libby's heart raced. Her fingers felt like icicles. How nice of them to bring her a birthday present. Finally she had the paper off and the box opened.

"Oooohhhh!" exclaimed Libby as she lifted out a light blue, weekend suitcase. "Oh, thank you!" Her hazel eyes were wide with pleasure.

"It's to use when you spend time with us," said Grandma, pecking Libby on her flushed cheek. "We thought maybe you'd like to come during spring vacation."

Tears pricked her eyelids as she clasped the handle of the suitcase. They really wanted her!

"We want you to come," said Grandpa. "We live in a small town, so it'll be different than you've known here or in the city."

"Oh, Libby!" cried Susan, clasping her slender hands together. "You'll love visiting them. We always have a lot of fun when we visit."

"And we have a lot of fun having you," said Grandma hugging Susan.

"Can I really go?" asked Libby, lifting begging eyes to Vera.

"Sure you can, Libby," said Vera happily.

"Then, I want to," said Libby, grinning from ear to ear. She would be like any other kid, visiting grandparents during vacation. Suddenly everything seemed right. She was happy. She was going to be happy forever!

SEVEN
The snowman

Libby flopped down on the ground and spread her arms and legs out, making the outline of an angel in the snow. Carefully she stood up, then jumped from it so that footprints wouldn't be near it. She smiled proudly as she brushed snow off her back. It was the best angel she'd made yet. She could hardly wait to show Susan. She could hear Susan and Kevin shouting with glee as they slid down the hill in back of the chicken house. She knew Goosy Poosy would be on the sled in front of Kevin.

Grandma and Grandpa were in town with Ben at Chuck's general store. Mom was in the house baking pies. Where was Toby? Libby looked around, frowning. He had been sliding with Kevin. She'd come back to the house so Toby could have fun. Today she wouldn't do anything to make him unhappy. She was happy, and wanted everyone else to be.

Apache Girl whinnied. Star answered. Libby looked toward the barn. The horses were walking around in the pen. Rex was flopped down in front of the barn door, his head resting on his paws. A movement at the side of the house caught Libby's attention. She turned. Toby was standing there, looking sad and lonely.

"Want to build a snowman, Toby?" called Libby cheerfully. This was just the perfect day to make friends. Today anything could happen!

Toby shook his head no and disappeared around the house.

Libby wouldn't allow it to make her feel bad. She would build a snowman herself. The best snowman in the world! Toby Smart could stay on the other side of the house and pout, but he'd miss out on a lot of fun!

The snow was just right for packing. Libby made a fat snowball, then rolled it across the yard and around her angel. The sun sparkled on the snow. Libby burst into song as she rolled the snowball around until it was just the size she wanted. She rubbed across the top of it, making it flat for the middle section. She spied Toby peeking around the corner of the house. She ignored him as she rolled another ball around the yard. Her cheeks were pink, her nose cold. A car drove past on the road.

The snowball was almost too large to pick up by herself. Finally she pushed it in place, then laughed with delight. Her mittens were soaked, her hands cold. She rolled the last snowball around and placed it as the head.

Toby was standing near the swing. Libby ignored him as she smoothed the snow until it looked like a big, fat snowman. She laughed. "Hi, Snowman. Are you Frosty? Will you come to life?"

She heard Toby laugh. Her heart skipped a beat. She knew something super would happen today.

"I need sticks for arms and stones for a face," she said, not looking at Toby. "You find the stones in the driveway, Toby, while I find the right sticks."

She didn't wait for an answer. She found sticks under the large oak in the front yard. "Just right," she said happily as she dashed back to the snowman. Toby was in the driveway searching for stones. Libby smiled.

"You're a good friend, Frosty," whispered Libby as she stuck the sticks in his arms. "I'm ready for the stones," she said. She smoothed the snow as she waited for Toby. Finally he walked to her and held out the stones. She took them without looking at him. If he didn't like her because she was ugly, she would not show him her face. Maybe then he wouldn't be afraid of her.

Finally she stepped back and surveyed her snowman. "He is beautiful," she said. "Thank you, Toby, for your help." She peeked at him. He was smiling at the snowman.

Dare she try something else with him? She hesitated, then shrugged. "Want me to push you on the swing?"

He backed away, then slowly nodded yes.

She waited until he was sitting in the swing, then she stood behind him and pushed him high.

"Stop it!" he shouted in terror. "Stop me!"

Libby grabbed him, jerking him to a stop. What a big baby! "You won't fall, you know," she said impatiently.

"You were trying to push me out," he yelled angrily.

"I was not!" she cried, her wet-mittened hands on her hips, her feet apart. "Just swing yourself. See if I care!" She turned and dashed toward the house. Now she'd ruined everything. She shouldn't have gotten upset

with him. Really, she should tell him she was sorry and explain patiently that she thought he wanted to go high in the swing. She turned to go back, then stopped. Toby was lunging against the snowman.

"Toby Smart!" she screamed, rushing across the yard. "Don't you dare knock down my snowman!" But she was too late. The snowman lay scattered around the yard.

Toby was staring defiantly up at her.

"Why did you do that?" she asked angrily, grabbing Toby's arm. "Why did you knock down my snowman?"

He jerked away from her. "I hate you, Janis," he said gruffly. He turned and raced away, then yelled over his shoulder. "I hate you!"

"My name is not Janis," she screamed as she ran after him. He ran over her angel. Just wait until she got her hands on him!

He dodged around a tree. "You're just pretending to be Libby," he said, his voice shaking with fright. "I know who you really are."

She stopped dead. "You are weird, Toby Smart! I am Elizabeth Gail Dobbs."

"Dobbs the Slob," cried Brenda Wilkens, running across the yard.

Libby glared at her. Who invited Brenda over? Or had she thought since she lived just down the road she could drop in anytime?

"Don't start trouble, Brenda," said Joe, following close behind his sister. "Hi, Libby. We came to go sliding."

"What are you doing to poor Toby?" asked Brenda, putting her arm around the boy. "What's the matter, Toby? Is Libby being mean again?"

Libby wanted to push her in the snow.

"Her name's not Libby," said Toby, his fists knotted hard. "She's only pretending that it is."

"You dope," said Libby, turning her back on him. So, who wanted to be friends?

"She doesn't have a name," said Brenda, laughing. "She's an aid kid."

"Come on, Libby," said Joe. "Let's go slide."

Libby ran at top speed toward the sliding hill where Susan and Kevin were still playing. She wouldn't think of Toby or of Brenda. She picked up her sled in back of the chicken house. She could hear Brenda and Toby talking and laughing behind her.

"Don't let them worry you," said Joe softly as he pulled his sled along beside her. "Let's have fun."

"I'll try," she said tiredly.

The trip up the hill seemed a mile long. Libby's legs ached. At the top she panted heavily until finally she caught her breath. What a long hill!

"Let's have a race," shouted Susan, her cheeks red, her eyes sparkling. "We'll line up here. Two on each sled."

"You ride with me, Libby," said Joe.

"OK," agreed Libby excitedly as she dropped her sled in place.

"Toby and I will ride together," said Brenda, holding the sled as Toby sat in place.

"It's a good thing Goosy Poosy stayed in the yard," said Kevin, laughing. "I don't think he'd want to race. Especially if we fell off."

"Everybody ready?" shouted Susan as Kevin climbed on the sled.

Libby looked to her right at Brenda and Toby, then

to her left at Kevin and Susan. This was going to be a good race.

"You get on in front, Libby," said Joe, holding the sled so it wouldn't fly down the hill alone.

Libby's knees almost touched her chin as she sat waiting for Susan to yell *go*. Libby clutched the rope and held her feet firmly on the guide bar. Joe sat close behind her, his arms around her waist.

"We'll beat 'em, Libby," he said excitedly. "Just keep it going straight down."

"Get ready. Get set. Go!" shouted Susan from her seat behind Kevin.

Libby's eyes sparkled excitedly as they sped down the long hill. Snow flicked against her face. She could hear the others shouting on either side. She just knew they were going to win. She leaned forward to increase speed. She could see the red, white, and blue of Toby's snowmobile suit flash past them. Oh no! Brenda and Toby were going to win. Her heart sank. Couldn't she ever win at anything?

Suddenly her sled hit a hard mound of snow, sending it bouncing toward Toby and Brenda.

"Watch out!" she yelled at the top of her lungs. "Brenda! Toby! Move over!"

"They aren't moving," cried Joe. "Libby, head off the track away from them."

"I'm trying!" she cried her voice cracking in fright. *Please, God,* she prayed urgently. *Help us.*

Just in time the sled swerved. Joe and Libby plowed into a pile of loose snow that sent them sprawling.

"You did that on purpose!" screamed Brenda, racing toward them before Libby could stand. "You made us lose. You made our sled tip over and Toby got full of snow."

Libby pushed herself up, brushed off the snow, and looked wildly around for Toby. Was he hurt? It would be terrible if she'd caused him to get hurt.

"It wasn't Libby's fault," said Joe as he wiped snow off his face. "She hit a block of ice or something."

"Are you all right?" asked Susan as she and Kevin dashed across the snowy hill toward them.

"We're fine," answered Joe as he brushed Toby off.

"Why'd you go off your track, Libby?" asked Kevin, his round face in a frown.

Libby wanted to shout and throw a fit, but she remembered that when she'd prayed, God had answered and kept them from colliding. No one had been hurt.

"Let's go to the house," said Libby hoarsely. "Maybe Mom will let me make cocoa for everyone." She caught the surprised look on Brenda's face. "You come, too, Brenda," Libby added, surprising herself more than anyone.

EIGHT
A talk with Grandpa

Libby sat cups of steaming cocoa in front of each person. Never had she felt this way! It was like being cold and uncared for, then being wrapped in a soft, warm blanket and cuddled close. God had actually answered her prayer! She felt so full of love that she thought she would burst.

She plopped a marshmallow in her cocoa, then carried it to the table. She knew Brenda was watching her closely. Libby looked right at her and smiled. Brenda blinked in surprise, her cup halfway to her mouth.

Libby sat beside Joe. He was talking to Susan about Apache Girl. Toby and Kevin were sipping their cocoa. Toby had a white glob on his lips where the melting marshmallow had stuck. Libby smiled at him. He looked quickly down at his cup. She didn't care. Something wounderful had happened on the sliding hill. Something she'd never forget.

Brenda took a sip of cocoa, then sat her cup down. "Did you open your puzzle box yet?" she asked innocently.

Libby knew that Brenda was trying to make her angry. "I haven't tried," she answered calmly.

"What's in it?" asked Joe excitedly, his dark eyes sparkling. "Everytime I think about it, I want to find your box and force it open. How can you stand not knowing what's in it?"

Libby shrugged, her heart beating faster. How she wished they would talk of something else!

"Maybe it's full of money," said Susan, her blue eyes bright, her fingers curled around her cup.

Libby looked sharply at Susan, surprised that Susan would join in the conversation. She knew how Libby felt.

"What if it is money?" continued Brenda excitedly. "Or diamonds! It could have almost anything in it." She looked at Libby, feverishly excited. "Get the box and I'll open it."

"No," whispered Libby hoarsely. What had happened to that good feeling she'd had just minutes before? She rubbed her damp palms down her jeans.

"Please, Libby," begged Kevin, leaning toward her in anticipation. "Get it and let's open in right now."

"We want to know what your dad sent you," said Susan, locking her fingers together.

Brenda jumped up. "Tell me where it is and I'll get it for you."

"She keeps it in her closet," said Kevin, squirming excitedly.

"I'll get it!" cried Brenda, heading for the door.

"No!" shouted Libby, grabbing her hard around the wrist and jerking her to a stop. "I don't want you to touch it." She turned to the others wildly. "And I don't want to talk about it anymore!"

"Hey, what's going on in here?" asked Grandpa, coming in the kitchen.

"Nothing," mumbled Libby, darting a look at the others and daring them to say anything. The smug look on Brenda's face startled her. Just what was Brenda up to?

"Mr. Johnson," said Brenda sweetly. "We were trying to help Libby with a problem she has. You know how independent she can be."

Libby wanted to strangle her.

"Maybe I can help you, Libby," said Grandpa kindly.

"Try, Grandpa," said Kevin, hurrying to his side. "Libby got a puzzle box from her real dad and it's full of secrets. She can't get it open."

"Bring it here," said Grandpa, grinning proudly. "I'm sure I could have it open in no time."

"She won't let us get it," said Brenda with an unhappy sigh. "I guess she doesn't want to bother us with it. But we really want to help."

"Oh, Brenda," said Joe in disgust. "It's not like that at all, Mr. Johnson."

Libby locked her fingers behind her back. What should she do now? Tears stung her eyelids. She knew if she tried to talk, she would burst out crying. No way would she cry in front of all of them.

"Maybe I should hear more from Libby," he said, looking at her expectantly. He stuck his hands in his pants pockets and jingled his money and keys.

Libby swallowed hard, but still couldn't say a word. She knew everyone was watching her, waiting to hear what she'd say. She felt hot all over, then cold.

Grandpa put an arm around her shoulders. "Come with me, young lady," he said gently. "The rest of you finish your cocoa and clean up the kitchen."

Libby could smell his after-shave lotion. It was the same kind that she sometimes smelled on Chuck.

Grandpa was just a little taller and leaner than Chuck. He had the same gentle touch. Libby found herself wanting to tell him exactly how she felt.

"Grandma and Vera are downstairs looking at something or other," said Grandpa, chuckling softly. "You and I'll go into the study and close the door and have us a long talk."

Libby sank gratefully to the couch, Grandpa right beside her. She blinked hard to keep the tears back.

"Take as long as you need," said Grandpa, his voice warm and caring. "Then I want to hear all about this mystery box of yours."

Libby looked at the fireplace. Someone had forgotten to clean out the ashes. She looked at Dad's big oak desk. Several papers were held in place by a large glass paperweight. Finally she was able to tell Grandpa about her read dad, the puzzle box, and the letters.

"Quite a story," said Grandpa thoughtfully. "I can see why it would be hard for you to care enough to open the box." He put his arm around her. "You've had a pretty hard life, Libby. But what's past is past." He lifted her hand, seeming to study it with the greatest care. "It isn't your dad you're hurting, you know."

Libby's eyes were glued to Grandpa's bony fingers.

"It's yourself," he continued softly. "That's what concerns me, honey. You must have a mighty big hurt inside you."

Tears filled Libby's eyes. She blinked hard. She would not cry!

"What hurt the most, Libby? His deserting you or his trying to come back into your life?"

Libby shrugged. She hadn't really thought about it.

"You must realize it wasn't your fault that he left home."

Hot tears streamed down her pale cheeks. In agony she leaned against Grandpa. "It must have been my fault," she said in a harsh, broken voice. "I know he hated me, that he thought I was ugly. He couldn't stand to be around me."

"There, there, honey," said Grandpa, patting her back as she sobbed against his shoulder. "I know that was hard for you to say. But, Elizabeth, it isn't true."

She lifted her face, her hazel eyes wide. Her hair was mussed, the tip of her nose red.

"It wasn't your fault. It wasn't you or your looks or your actions. It was his unhappiness with himself, his dissatisfaction that make him leave you and his wife. He couldn't face his responsibilities as a father and husband.

"There are people like that. I've seen them, been friends with them." Grandpa cleared his throat. "Some of them mature, some don't. Your father must have matured enough to get in touch with you. If he'd lived, he might have found the courage to come visit you, even take you with him. None of his actions are your fault. You didn't cause any of it."

Libby couldn't grasp what he was saying. It had to be her fault. It had been her fault with everyone else that had rejected her. She couldn't even count the number of foster homes she'd had. She was still with the Johnsons because they had prayed for a girl, and God had given her to them.

Grandpa wiped her tears with his big white hanky. "Maybe if you opened the box and found the secrets inside, you'd understand your dad and be able to lose those bitter feelings you have for him. When a person allows bitterness and hatred to stay inside, those feelings push out any *good* feelings the person might have." He rubbed her hair away from her face. "Have you ever seen a rotten potato in a sack of potatoes? It smells horrible, and it makes the potatoes touching it turn rotten and smelly."

Libby remembered just the other day when she'd taken out potatoes for supper and found a rotten one. She wrinkled her nose. It had smelled so bad her stomach had turned. For a while she'd thought she was going to be sick.

"Bad feelings inside you are like that," said Grandpa seriously. "They touch your good feelings and turn them bad."

Libby could picture a bag inside her filled with all kinds of feelings. Were her bad feelings affecting everything? Would she turn rotten inside if she allowed the bad feelings to stay? How could she get rid of them? It had been easy enough to toss out the rotten potato. But how could she toss out a bad feeling? Hesitantly she asked Grandpa what she should do.

"Do you think Jesus can answer prayer?" Grandpa answered her question with a question.

Libby thought of the prayer he'd answered just a while ago, and nodded yes.

"We'll pray right now, then," he said softly.

Libby bowed her head next to his. As he prayed aloud for her, she prayed silently.

"I think we both feel better, don't you?" asked

Grandpa, wiping tears from his blue eyes.

"Yes," she said, finally able to smile. She wanted to wait until she was alone before she really found out her new feelings toward Dad.

"If you want help with that secret box of yours, just ask me," said Grandpa, his eyes twinkling as he stood up. "I don't think your dad would care at all if your grandpa helped you."

Libby smiled hesitantly. Did she want to open the box? It would be nice if Grandpa could help her.

Just then the study door opened. "Oh, here you are, Libby," said Vera with a smile. "It's time to do chores. Dad said you could put Chester in the other barn."

"Who's Chester?" asked Grandpa.

"One of the animals that Libby's been doctoring," said Vera. "She's very good with them."

Libby grinned, feeling wonderful. "Do you want to come with me, Grandpa? I'll introduce you to Chester."

"Give me a few minutes to put on some work clothes," he said happily. "I want a look at Snowball, too."

"You won't believe how she's grown," said Vera as they walked out of the study.

"Maybe I'll go for a long ride," said Grandpa, winking at Libby.

Libby giggled as she hurried to the back porch for outdoor clothes. Maybe after chores she'd get her box out of the closet and open it, at least try.

"Libby! Libby, hurry," cried Kevin as he poked his red face in the back door. Cold air streamed in, chilling Libby.

"Why?" she asked as she grabbed her coat.

"Chester's out. We've got to get him before he gets on the road."

Libby hurried, the secret box completely out of her thoughts.

NINE
The sleigh ride

Don't daydream, Libby," called Ben as he walked the big matched team of grays from the barn. "Help me hitch Jack and Dan to the sleigh."

Libby pulled herself back from preparing for Kevin's school class to come for a sleigh ride around the farm. She'd been remembering how they'd all laughed as they'd chased down Chester, then put him back in the barn. Even Grandpa had helped, acting like a cowboy, waving his hat and yelling, "Ya hoo, ya ya."

Libby laughed again as she worked with Ben. It had been so nice having Grandma and Grandpa there. They'd gone home late Sunday afternoon.

"Remember all we talked about, Elizabeth girl," Grandpa had said when he'd kissed her good-bye.

"I will, Grandpa," she promised. She had thought about her box, but she hadn't had a chance to try to open it. Maybe she really wasn't quite ready to.

Noisy kids clamoring off the big black and yellow school bus sent Libby scurrying off to get the last robe to put in the sleigh. She picked up the heavy robe, closed the tack room door, and locked it. Vera had said it would keep the kids from getting into trouble. She said one year that Susan's class had come out for the day, Larry Grayton had gone in the tack room and taken saddles down, scattered several items around, and even opened the medicine chest. Vera didn't want that to happen again.

"Hurry, Libby," called Kevin, rushing into the barn to find her. "Ben is ready to load the first group in the sleigh." Kevin's face shone with excitement. "Mrs. Main said she would ride with each group."

"Did Susan take her group to the ice pond?" asked Libby as she hurried along beside Kevin, who was running every other step to keep up.

"They're going now. Toby's going with Susan, and Mom told Mrs. Main she'd keep an eye on the kids left here while you and Ben take them in the sleigh."

"Are you going first trip?" asked Libby, smiling as she caught his excitement.

"Yes. Mrs. Main wants me to."

The gray horses trampled the snow, blowing out their breaths loudly. Bells jingled merrily.

Libby called for the kids to climb in and she covered them with the heavy robe. Four kids sat in the middle seat. Mrs. Main and two kids sat in the backseat. Libby climbed in front with Kevin and Ben. She looked back eagerly to see that all was ready. "Hang on. We're going," called Libby, laughing gaily, her hazel eyes sparkling.

"Get up," commanded Ben, slapping the horses on the back. Jack and Dan stepped along briskly, their bells jingling merrily over the loud shouts from the kids in the sleigh and the others at the pond.

Libby lifted her face to the overcast sky. What a beautiful day! Right now she would have been in English class studying boring grammar. She smiled at Kevin and he smiled back. Good old Kevin. Too bad he couldn't have his class come out every day.

Some of the kids started singing "Jingle Bells." Libby laughed and joined in. Here it was almost March and they were singing "Jingle Bells"!

Libby glanced over her shoulder and saw the terror on a little brown-eyed girl's face. What could she say to take away the girl's fear? Not long ago she wouldn't have noticed anyone's feelings but her own.

Leaning close to Kevin she whispered. "Who's the girl just back of you? The one in the red-checkered snowsuit."

"Melinda Bender," whispered Kevin, frowning. "Why?"

Libby shrugged, then turned to Melinda. "I can remember the first time I rode on the wagon and the sleigh," she said cheerfully. "I thought I was going to sail right out and land on my head. But I didn't. Once I got used to the motion, I liked it." She noticed Melinda relaxing a little. "We've taken lots of people on sleigh rides and not one fell out. Ben has a Christmas tree business, and I helped him this year."

Libby explained how she and Ben took the customers to the spot where Ben had Christmas trees planted, then allowed the customer to choose a tree and cut it. Ben would load it in back of the sleigh, and as they all rode back they would sing Christmas songs.

"It was really fun," said Libby, smiling because Melinda Bender was smiling and no longer afraid.

Libby turned around, a warm, contented feeling

spreading through her. It felt good to help others.

Jack and Dan walked briskly past the grove of trees and through the pasture where the yearlings grazed during the spring and summer. After the March thaw Chuck had said they would all help drive the steers back. Libby flushed with anticipation, picturing herself astride Apache Girl, driving the cattle and yelling like Grandpa had yelled at Chester.

"Quick!" exclaimed Ben, his eyes bright on Libby. "Look over there."

Libby gasped in delight at the sight of five white-tailed deer. She turned to motion for the others to see, then watched the deer spring across the hill, down, and into the forest of pine, oak, and poplar. Libby let out her breath in a long sigh of pleasure.

A weak sun came out, shining enough to brighten the countryside. How would it feel during the spring? Tears pricked Libby's eyelids as she realized how close she'd come to missing spring in the country. Now she was here at the Johnsons' farm to stay. Please, God, let it be true.

After the third trip with the third group of boys and girls, Libby was glad to take them out for lunch. Vera and Susan had made chili. How good it tasted with soda crackers crumbled up in it. The corners of her mouth stung and her nose started to run. She ate three bowls anyway.

"Do you want Susan to go on the sleigh this last trip?" asked Vera as she stood beside Libby outside the back door.

"Does she want to go?" asked Libby, hoping the answer would be no.

"She would rather stay and skate with the kids,"

answered Vera, pulling on her red gloves. "But she said if you wanted to stay, she'd go with Ben."

"I want to go on the sleigh," said Libby, beaming. How could anyone choose ice skating over riding in the sleigh?

"Toby's riding this trip," said Vera thoughtfully. "Can you handle that?"

Libby looked across the crowded yard at the boy dressed in a red, white, and blue snowmobile suit. Toby had kept out of her way lately, and she hadn't done anything to upset him. "I won't even look at him," she said.

"Oh, I don't think it's that bad," said Vera, laughing as she walked across the yard with Libby. "You've been a big help today, Libby. Thank you. Mrs. Main told me how you talked Melinda out of being afraid. It was very kind of you."

Libby felt ten feet tall.

"Ben said the sleigh rides this year are better than any other year." Vera slid her arm around Libby's waist. "I'm so glad you belong to us."

"Me too," said Libby with feeling. How awful if she lived in town with a family that couldn't stand the sight of her!

"I see Ben's ready with Jack and Dan," said Vera, hugging Libby. "We'll see you later."

Libby felt as if she was floating to the sleigh. "Climb in, everyone," she said.

"Toby can ride up with us," said Ben as he climbed up.

"I can get up myself," said Toby sharply as Libby moved to help him.

"OK," she said with a shrug.

"Will we see deer?" asked a boy with chili smeared across his cheek.

"Maybe," answered Libby as she climbed into the seat. "We'll watch closely." She tried to ignore Toby as he huddled as close to Ben as he could.

Mrs. Main started the boys and girls on "Jingle Bells" again as the sleigh glided over the firmly packed track. The sun was a little warmer. Maybe in another week the snow would be melted away.

As they were coming back about twenty-five minutes later, Toby moaned and grabbed Ben's arm. "I'm sick," he gasped, his face deathly white.

"Take care of him, Libby," said Ben as he called the horses to a stop.

Libby leaped down, then reached up for Toby.

"I'm going to throw up," said Toby, leaning weakly against Libby.

"I'll hold you," said Libby gently.

"Do you need any help?" asked Mrs. Main in concern.

"I can manage," said Libby, sounding surer than she felt. She waited until Toby was finished, then wiped his mouth. "Will you be all right now?"

He nodded weakly.

"I'll help you back up," she said, half lifting him up beside Ben.

"We'll be home soon," said Ben. "Just hang on, Toby."

"Lean on me," said Libby, putting her arm around Toby and pulling him close. "You'll be just fine."

Ben clucked to the horses, and Mrs. Main started another song.

"Close your eyes, Toby," said Libby softly. "Think of

something pleasant. Think about all the gifts you'll get day after tomorrow for your birthday." She did that a lot. If she was too upset, she'd let her mind drift off until it found something good to think about, then she'd think on it until she felt better. It worked, too.

A few minutes later Ben stopped Jack and Dan in the yard. The kids scrambled out, shouting with pleasure. Libby jumped down, then helped Toby.

He looked up at her, his eyes large and troubled. "You were nice to me today, Janis, but I still don't like you."

Libby gasped. Janis! Not again. Before she could say anything, he raced to the house.

"Why did he call you Janis?" asked Ben, frowning after Toby.

"I don't know," said Libby in a puzzled voice. "He did it the other day, too. Something is wrong with him."

"It's sure funny," said Ben. He shrugged. "Help me unhitch Jack and Dan, Libby."

As she worked she heard the whistle that Mrs. Main used to call all the boys and girls back to the bus. It was time for them to go back to school. Kevin didn't have to. Libby watched him hopping around in the snow as the others climbed on the bus. Toby stood with Vera, telling all of them good-bye. Libby frowned. Was Toby afraid of her because she was ugly? Or, was something wrong with Toby?

Libby walked beside Ben as he walked Jack and Dan to the barn. Should she forget the entire incident, or should she talk to Chuck about it?

"Grab the harness, Libby," said Ben sharply as he staggered under the bulky load.

Libby jerked her attention back to helping Ben. The joy had gone out of the day. Tiredly she helped Ben hang the harness in the tack room. Just what could she do about Toby?

TEN
Happy birthday, Toby Smart

Libby pulled out the sugar canister while Susan took the eggs out of the refrigerator. Vera already had the butter in the mixing bowl.

"Put one and one-third cups sugar in, Libby," said Vera as she turned the mixer down from high to second.

Carefully Libby measured it out, then dumped it in. She liked the way the butter seemed to eat the sugar right up.

"Susan, scrape in that melted chocolate," said Vera, looking over her shoulder at Susan. Vera smiled at both girls. "Toby will have the best birthday cake in the world with the three of us working on it."

Libby watched the yellow mixture streak with chocolate, then suddenly turn completely brown. How good the cake would taste! She'd like a great big piece right now.

"Libby, break four eggs in a cup," said Vera as she scraped around the bowl with a rubber spatula.

Carefully Libby broke the eggs in the cup, taking

extra care not to drop in a piece of shell. Would Toby want to eat his birthday cake if he knew she had helped bake it? He'd probably take it out and feed it to Rex.

She had told Chuck about Toby calling her Janis. It kind of made her feel prickly all over for him to call her Janis. Who was Janis? Libby shrugged. Maybe Chuck was right—Toby had only forgotten her name.

"The flour, Susan," said Vera, nudging her daughter. "Hey, we forgot to turn on the oven."

"I'll turn it on," said Libby, quickly reaching for the dial before Susan could. "Is 350 degrees right?" Vera said it was, so Libby turned the dial slowly, enjoying every second of it. Susan wrinkled her nose at Libby, then smiled.

"How's Snowball today?" asked Vera as she wiped her fingers on a paper towel.

"OK," said Libby. Had she remembered to put the salve away after she'd rubbed it on Snowball's shoulder?

"Star really bit her hard," said Susan, leaning on the counter.

"I guess horses can be disagreeable just like people," said Vera, grinning from Susan to Libby.

Libby looked sheepishly at Susan. They'd been screaming at each other just minutes before about who was going to help bake the birthday cake. It was settled by both of them helping.

"At least I didn't bite Libby," said Susan, giggling.

"But you sure felt like it," said Libby, giggling, too. "And I wouldn't want to use that smelly salve on myself."

They worked together in the cheery, light green

73

kitchen until the cake was baked and cooling on the rack.

"While I fry the chicken, you girls peel potatoes," said Vera as she mixed flour, salt, and pepper in a bowl.

Immediately Libby thought of her talk with Grandpa. Did she have any of her bad feelings left? She tried to concentrate her thoughts on Frank Dobbs, but her love for Chuck Johnson kept pushing the thoughts away. As she peeled the potatoes she forced her mind to stay on her real dad. Her heart seemed to stop. A hard knot tightened her stomach. She just couldn't think of him now. Maybe when she was alone in her room, where she could cry if she felt like it, she could sort out her feelings.

Just then the phone rang. Susan whispered something to Libby as Vera answered. At the excitement in Vera's voice the girls turned to watch her. It must be terrific news. Vera pushed her blonde hair back, then fumbled with the gold chain around her slender neck. Her blue eyes sparkled. What could be that wonderful?

Libby and Susan cut the potatoes into small pieces, dropped them in a large pan, and then set them on the burner.

Vera hung up the phone, then stood with her fingers at her lips, her eyes sort of glazed.

"What it is, Mom?" asked Susan in concern.

"It must be super," said Libby, her fingers locked together in front of her.

"That was Miss Miller," whispered Vera, her hand over her heart.

Libby turned pale. What had the caseworker said to

74

affect Vera this way? Libby's mouth felt cotton dry. She swallowed hard.

"I really should wait to tell Dad first," said Vera in a happy daze.

"Tell us!" cried Susan, bobbing up and down.

Libby didn't know if she wanted to hear. It might be happy for them, sad for her. What had Miss Miller said? Suddenly Libby just had to know. She would die if she couldn't hear right this minute what Miss Miller had said. "Please, please, tell us," she begged, her hazel eyes wide in alarm.

Vera took a deep breath, then slowly let it out. "We have permission to apply to adopt Toby! We really get to adopt him!"

Libby blinked back sharp tears. It wasn't fair! She should have been the one to be adopted first. Libby turned on the water and let it run over her hands. She couldn't let Mom and Susan see how upset she was. They were chattering away, too happy to notice Libby.

Libby turned off the water, fighting against her tears. "I'm . . . I'm going to check Snowball," she said, forcing her voice to sound natural.

In a flash she grabbed her coat off the hook next to Dad's.

The air was colder. Maybe it would snow again tonight. Libby stopped, listening to the sound of a car. Was Dad coming home now? The car whizzed past. Libby rushed to the barn, her heart racing wildly.

She hugged Snowball, muttering softly and brokenheartedly how she should be the one to be adopted, not Toby Smart, the freckle-faced, red-haired, thumb-sucking, scaredy-cat!

Why wouldn't Mother sign the papers to give the

Johnsons permission to adopt her? Did Mother think she could come home from Australia this year or next and take Libby back? That would be the worst thing in the whole world!

Libby rubbed the back of her hand across her nose, then down her jeans. Tears slid down her pale cheeks. Her brown hair was mussed and had pieces of hay sticking in it.

"Libby!" It was Ben. "What're you doing in here now?"

Libby quickly brushed away her tears, then turned to Ben. "I wanted to see Snowball."

"She'll be OK," said Ben, stooping to have a closer look at the bite on Snowball's shoulder. "I guess Star needs to go to bed early for a month!"

Libby giggled. She'd been punished like that several times since she'd come here to live. "I know she'll be all right," said Libby, looking lovingly at her white filly. "I just like to touch her and think about her being mine."

"I know how you feel," said Ben as they walked slowly to the door. "I feel the same about Star." Ben clicked off the lights and they stepped outside. It was almost dark enough to require the yard light.

Rex barked and raced to them. As Libby bent to hug him, he licked her cheek. She turned her face for him to lick her other cheek.

Pickup truck lights stabbed through the dimness, bouncing off the oak in the front yard, then off the big maple to the side of the house.

"Dad's home," said Ben, waving as the green pickup drove around by the garage, then stopped.

Libby held back as Ben dashed to greet Chuck.

Would he be so excited about adopting Toby that he'd forget all about her? Would he stop having the heart-to-heart chats that she enjoyed so much?

"Come here, Elizabeth," called Chuck cheerfully, his arm around Ben.

Her heart leaping happily, Libby dashed to him, almost bursting with joy as he put his other arm around her. She and Ben were only half a head shorter than Chuck. He was heavier built. Ben and Libby were almost toothpick thin.

"I brought home chocolate and vanilla ice cream for Toby's party," said Chuck. "Did you get the drawing kit wrapped, Elizabeth?"

She nodded. She hadn't put her name on it, though. If Toby knew the drawing kit was from her, he'd probably burn it in the trash.

"Kevin and I got him a model airplane and car," said Ben, explaining excitedly exactly what each model was.

"I smell fried chicken," said Chuck as they hung up their coats on the back porch. "I'm hungry enough to eat ten chickens."

"But leave room for cake," said Libby. "Susan and I helped bake it." She didn't think she could enjoy the chicken or the chocolate cake and ice cream. Maybe she'd never eat anything again. She'd just melt away into nothing. And nobody would even notice.

It was hard to pretend to enjoy the birthday supper. Every time she looked at Toby she wanted to rip the freckles right off his face. When he laughed or talked she wanted to yell at him to shut up. Twice Vera looked at her sharply, and then Libby would try harder to laugh with the others.

Toby blew out his nine candles, then immediately stuck his thumb in his mouth. What a baby!

Toby opened his gifts as Vera cut the cake. To Libby's surprise Toby liked the drawing kit the best. For a minute it made her feel better.

Everyone jumped when the front doorbell rang.

"Now, who could that be?" asked Chuck as he started for the hall.

"I hope he hurries back so we can tell the *big* news," said Susan squirming even more than Kevin usually did.

Libby looked at her plate of ice cream and cake. She'd choke if she had to take one bite.

"Look who came to bring Toby a present," said Chuck, herding Brenda and Joe into the dining room.

Libby bit her lip to keep from screaming and screaming. Brenda looked right through her, then smiled brightly at Toby Smart. No—Toby Johnson. Libby coughed to cover the sob that escaped.

"Here, Toby," said Brenda, handing him a box wrapped paper covered with Charlie Brown and Snoopy. "Happy birthday."

Joe stood beside Ben's chair, smiling happily.

"Thanks," said Toby, beaming as he ripped off the paper. "It's great. Just great!" He held up the paint-by-number picture of boys playing football.

Did Toby like football? How could he play with his thumb in his mouth? Libby almost laughed at the thought.

"*Now,* Mom?" asked Susan excitedly.

"What?" asked Chuck, looking quickly at Vera.

She smiled warmly at Chuck, then at Toby. "This is

the best surprise yet," said Vera, her blue eyes sparkling. "Miss Miller called today to say we can apply for adoption."

"For Libby?" asked Kevin excitedly.

Libby thought she'd die.

"For Toby," said Vera, kissing Toby's freckled cheek.

The happiness on Chuck's face was more than Libby had anticipated. How she wanted to run to her room and stay there forever. She looked up and caught the knowing look on Brenda's face. Libby's stomach flipped. She locked her hands together in her lap. If Brenda said one thing to embarrass her or cause the others to feel bad, she'd sock her right in the mouth. She would! And love doing it!

She was glad when Brenda and Joe left. She was glad when dishes were done. During family devotions she sat quietly as Vera read the fifth chapter of the adventure story. She didn't listen as Chuck read three Scriptures. It was Kevin's turn to pray. At least he always said a short prayer. When he thanked God that they could adopt Toby, Libby pressed her hands against her closed eyes until they hurt.

Finally she was able to escape to her room. She flung herself across her bed, her face buried against Pinky's soft neck. But the tears didn't come. She'd fought to hold them back all evening, and now they refused to fall.

She leaped up, pacing the floor from the desk to the big, red hassock and back. Maybe something would happen that they couldn't adopt Toby. Maybe the judge wouldn't allow it. Maybe Toby would decide he didn't like them. Maybe she could do something really mean to Toby to make him leave. She stopped short, her hands over her mouth, her eyes wide. What was she thinking? What a terrible, terrible person she was. How could anyone love her? How could God love her?

She closed her eyes tight, her heart aching. "I'm sorry, Jesus," she whispered in agony. "I'm really sorry. Help me."

A sound from the hallway startled her. Chuck would be in to say good-night in a few minutes. She couldn't face him. Not yet.

Wildly she pulled off her jeans and shirt, flinging them into the red hamper near the closet. She slipped her nightgown over her head, then got under the covers.

She closed her eyes tight. No, that wouldn't work. Kevin pulled that trick when he wanted you to think he was asleep. He thought the tighter you closed your eyes, the more asleep you looked.

She turned on her right side and closed her eyes until the lashes barely touched her cheeks. She waited, forcing her body to relax.

He opened the door, flicked on the light, and called her named softly. Finally he turned off the light and closed her door.

She sighed in relief, her eyes wide open. Tomorrow she could face him. Tomorrow things would be better. She would be better because she was going to face herself.

Slowly she pushed back the sheet and cover and sat up. She would get down the puzzle box and try to open it.

With clammy hands she turned the knob on her closet. She dare not think, only act.

She reached for the box. It was gone. Gone! Who took it? Not Susan or Ben or Kevin. Certainly not Chuck or Vera.

Libby clenched her fists at her sides. It had to be Toby. Just wait until she got her hands on him!

ELEVEN
Where's Toby?

Libby crept down the hall to Toby's room. It had been hard to wait until she was sure everyone was asleep.

Cautiously she opened his door and slipped in. His night-light made enough light for her to see him fast asleep, his arms flung out, his mouth open. Her mouth tightened in a long, thin line.

She jerked him by the shoulders. "Wake up, Toby," she hissed, her face almost touching his. "Wake up, Toby! What did you do with my box?"

His eyes opened wide in terror. He cringed from her, whimpering in fright.

She shook him again. "Where is my box? My puzzle box?"

He opened his mouth wide, but before he could scream, she pressed her hand over it. "Don't you dare! If you make one sound that will wake the others, I'll slap you hard. Understand?"

He nodded, shivering uncontrollably.

Slowly she pulled her hand away. "Where is it?"

"I don't know," he whispered hoarsely.

She slapped him hard across the cheek, leaving fin-gerprints. "Tell me!"

Tears slid down his cheeks. His face was distorted with terror.

Libby lifted her hand to slap him again, then stopped in horror. What was she doing? What was wrong with her? How could she slap Toby? Her heart raced as she saw the finger marks on his cheeks. Oh, how she must have hurt him! Why hadn't she asked Dad or Mom to get the box back from Toby? Slowly she straightened up. "Go back to sleep, Toby," she said weakly. "I'm really sorry for hitting you. I'm sorry!"

He cringed against the pillow, shaking so hard the bed creaked, his eyes locked on her.

Tiredly Libby opened the door and left. Her shoulders drooped as she padded down the hall to her room, ashamed beyond words for what she'd done to Toby.

It took her hours to get to sleep.

"Libby! Libby, wake up."

Libby turned over and opened her heavy eyelids. "What's wrong, Susan?" she asked in a groggy voice.

"Toby is missing! He's gone! Disappeared!"

Libby sat up, suddenly wide awake, her heart racing.

"Mom went to call him for school, and he's gone," said Susan, starting to cry. "Libby, get up and help us look for him."

Had he run away to get away from her? With awk-ward fingers she pulled on her clothes. She thought she was going to be sick. She took a deep breath, then raced to Toby's room where the others were.

Vera was crying against Chuck's shoulder. They were all still in night clothes except for Libby and Ben.

"He may still be in the house somewhere," said

Chuck, frowning. "We'll go downstairs and each take a room and hunt."

Quietly they filed down. Libby jumped as the grandfather clock struck seven. One more hour before the school bus came.

"Libby, check the basement," said Chuck, running his fingers through his already mussed red hair.

Libby rushed away as Chuck sent the others out. Why would Toby be in the basement? If he'd run away, wouldn't he go outdoors where he could really run away? Maybe Chuck knew that, but he wanted to make sure first. Libby knew Chuck was going to look for footprints in the new fallen snow.

Feeling sicker by the minute, Libby looked throughout the basement, even in the storage area that you could only crawl into.

Reluctantly Libby walked upstairs to the family room where she heard Vera and Kevin. They looked up hopefully. She shook her head no, her shoulders sagging. Why hadn't she stayed away from Toby? She couldn't keep quiet about it. She just *couldn't*. But her tongue stuck to the roof of her mouth, and the words wouldn't come out.

One by one the others came in, each looking frightened and unhappy.

"There's not a sign of fresh tracks in the new snow," said Chuck, rubbing his wide forehead. "If he left the house, he left before the snow fell."

"I looked out about eleven-thirty and it was snowing then," said Vera hoarsely. "Do you suppose he ran away because he didn't want to be adopted by us?"

"Now, Vera," said Chuck, hugging her close. "You know how happy he was about us being his family." He brushed her hair away from her face. "There has to be a reason for him leaving, and he had to leave before eleven-thirty."

But Libby knew he hadn't. It had been five minutes to twelve when she'd gone to his room. She opened her mouth, determined to tell. But the words stuck in her throat.

Toby had to be in the house. He had to be!

"God knows where Toby is," said Chuck. He cleared his throat. "Let's ask him to help us find Toby."

Libby couldn't bear to stay in the room. Quietly she slipped away as Chuck prayed. What would they think of her if they knew what she'd done?

Quietly she slipped into Toby's room. She glanced at the blue spread, hanging half off the bed. The Charlie Brown sheet was off in another direction. She knew something was different about the bed. She gasped. Toby's bright blue nylon blanket was missing. She frowned as she walked around the room. She spied the blanket sticking out from under the bed. Her heart raced wildly. Could Toby be under the bed?

Libby held her breath as she peeked under. Sure enough. Toby was fast asleep, rolled up in the blanket, his thumb stuck in his mouth. Should she wake him? No! Never! He would scream and carry on if he saw her.

Who would have thought he'd be right in his own room under his own bed? How long had it taken him to get back to sleep after she left him? Had he stayed awake, scared to death, for hours and hours? The noise they all made earlier hadn't awakened him. Poor Toby.

Poor Libby. She sniffed hard, fighting against the tears. She had to tell them she'd found him.

They were still standing together in the family room when she walked in.

"He's . . . he's under his bed asleep," she said barely above a whisper. She wanted to sink through the floor as they stared at her in surprise. Then they all moved at once, rushing up the stairs to see Toby for themselves.

In a daze Libby followed them up. She heard Chuck telling the others that they'd let the little boy sleep.

"He must have had a nightmare," said Chuck as they left the room and he closed the door.

"I'll check on him from time to time," said Vera softly. "Kids, get your school clothes on while I fix breakfast."

Libby was anxious to get away from their excited exclamations on how she'd found Toby. She didn't want them to think she was great. She was the worst person in the whole world. She deserved to be kicked out and placed in a home where she would be beaten twice a day and fed bread crusts and powdered milk.

It was a relief to get to school and lose herself among the other kids in her room. She studied hard to keep from thinking about what she'd done. She participated in English class for the first time since she'd been there. She just had to keep her mind off how bad she'd been.

On the bus going home Libby sat next to a little punk named Lefty Babcock because the only other seat available was beside Susan.

She had three bruises on her arm where he pinched her by the time he hopped off the bus. Pinches were better that listening to Susan going on and on about how terrific she was for finding Toby.

Libby looked out the window as the bus stopped to let off Brenda and Joe. The Wilkenses' colonial house stood beautifully on a hill just up from the Johnsons' farm.

"I'm glad Toby had such a nice birthday," said Brenda, stopping at Libby's seat. "I could see how much you enjoyed it." Then she laughed.

Libby held her breath and knotted her fists. That Brenda!

"Hurry off, Wilkens," ordered the bus driver sternly as he looked over his shoulder.

"Libby grabbed me and wouldn't let me pass," said Brenda, tossing her long, black hair over her slender shoulder. She smiled triumphantly at Libby before she hurried away.

Libby slid down in her seat. Brenda was terrible, but *she* was worse, a whole lot worse!

TWELVE
One more letter

Slowly Libby walked up the long driveway. Had Toby told on her? What would happen if he had? Maybe she should confess her part. She choked. How could she tell? She couldn't! Unhappily she looked at the house.

"Why are you so slow, Libby?" asked Susan as she waited by the garage for Libby.

"I want to be alone," said Libby tiredly. Just how long would this be her home?

"Why?" asked Susan in surprise. "Did Brenda do something to you again?"

"What does it matter?" said Libby, pulling open the back door. Where was Toby? Was Vera waiting with Toby, ready to pounce on her? What would be her punishment? Would they hate her? She wouldn't blame them if they did. She hated herself.

From lack of sleep the night before, Libby found it hard to keep her eyes open as she automatically changed her school clothes, had a snack, and did chores. She hadn't seen Toby since morning. Was he staying out of her way?

"You're very quiet, Libby," said Vera as Libby slid onto the piano bench to do her lessons.

"I'm tired," said Libby listlessly.

"Honey, I hope you're not upset because we're able to adopt Toby," said Vera, her hands resting lightly on Libby's shoulders.

Libby stiffened.

"You know we can't adopt you yet." Vera kissed the top of Libby's head. "But we won't give up hoping. You're our girl, Elizabeth Gail, even if your last name isn't Johnson. You belong to us. We love you. We'll always love you."

Libby burst into tears. She covered her face with her hands, her thin shoulders shaking with sobs. They wouldn't love her if they knew what she'd done to Toby.

"Libby, honey," said Vera in concern as she tried to turn to Libby to her. "What is it?"

Libby fought against her tears until finally she had them under control. "I'm just tired," she whispered hoarsely.

"Skip practice tonight, then," said Vera, studying Libby thoughtfully. "Why don't you rest before Dad comes home."

Libby pushed herself up, the corners of her mouth drooping, tears sparkling in her eyes. "I think I will. I'll practice after supper."

"Did something happen in school today that upset you?" asked Vera as Libby walked listlessly toward the stairs.

Libby shook her head no.

"Mom! Mom, look what I painted," said Toby as he rushed in. He stopped dead at the sight of Libby. Slowly he backed until he was against the wall. His eyes were full of terror. He popped his thumb in his mouth.

Vera rushed to him as Libby fled upstairs.

Toby was more afraid of her than ever. Could she blame him?

Libby flung herself down on her bed and beat her fists against her pillow. She couldn't stand feeling like this. She had to tell Dad what she'd done. Her heart seemed to stop beating. She sat up tiredly. How could she tell Dad? She rubbed her hair back, then dropped her hand to her lap. She would wait until just the right time, and she'd tell him. A sob escaped, then another. She would not cry!

Slowly she walked to the bathroom and washed her face. It helped. She made a face at her reflection.

"Libby!" called Susan from downstairs. "Come here."

She probably needed help with her math. At least it would be something nice she could do. She'd done enough bad to last forever.

"Look, Libby," said Susan, holding out an envelope.

"The mailman left it at our house," said Joe Wilkens, smiling warmly at Libby. "I brought it right over as soon as I saw it."

Libby took it, knowing it was another letter from Dad. She didn't hate him anymore. She really understood why he'd left her. All she had to do was look in a mirror or think of her own actions and know he'd left to get away from her. It hadn't been his fault, but hers.

"Are you going to read it?" asked Susan excitedly.

"Sure," said Libby with a tired sigh. "Thanks, Joe, for bringing it."

"That's OK," he answered, grinning. "Have you tried to open your box?"

"No." She couldn't tell them the box was missing until she talked to Chuck.

"I can't wait until you open it," said Joe, stuffing his hands into his pockets. "Brenda and I talk a lot about the secrets inside. We've guessed lots of things. I can't wait to find out what's really in it."

"Me neither," said Susan, her ponytails bobbing furiously. "It must be something really great."

A shiver ran up and down Libby's back. Maybe there was something really terrific inside the box. When Dad got the box back from Toby, she'd really try to open it.

"Open the letter, Libby!" cried Susan, shaking Libby's arm hard.

Libby decided what she wanted to do. First, she'd get the box, then try to open it. Then, she'd read the new letter from Dad. Really, that would be the best. "I want to read my letter by myself later," she said to Susan and Joe. "But I will tell you what it says." She didn't like to see the disappointment on their faces.

Suddenly she was anxious to talk to Chuck. She wanted to tell him what she'd done to Toby. What did it matter if she had to go to bed early for a while? A wave of nausea swept over her as she thought of the very worst he could do to her. He could send her back to Miss Miller to find her a new home. No! She wouldn't think of that. Hadn't Vera said just a while ago that they all loved her and wanted her?

Later, Libby sat in the study across from Chuck. She was trying very hard to stay calm. He looked at her earnestly, waiting for her to tell him why she'd needed so desperately to talk to him alone.

"Is it really that bad, Elizabeth?" asked Chuck softly

as he leaned across his desk, his hazel eyes studying her. "You know you can talk to me about anything."

"I . . . I don't know how to say it," she said in a strangled voice. This was going to he hard, harder than she realized.

"Just start," he said, leaning back and smiling. He rubbed his red hair back, but it flopped again over his wide forehead.

Libby looked down at her faded blue sneakers, then at her hands locked together in her lap. "Toby took my box and I hit him," she said in a rush.

"How do you know Toby took it?" asked Chuck calmly.

"Because it's gone and no one else in this family would have," she said, her eyes begging him to understand and be kind.

"OK. You found out he took it and then what?"

Libby took a deep breath and told Chuck the story. "I . . . I didn't mean to scare him so badly," she finished, tears in her eyes.

Chuck was quiet for so long, Libby wanted to die. She twisted her fingers until her knuckles cracked. She rubbed her foot up and down her leg. What was he thinking?

"I'll call Toby in," said Chuck, pushing himself up.

"He's too scared of me to talk," said Libby, following Chuck to the study door.

"I'll talk and you sit quietly," said Chuck squeezing Libby.

Libby smiled shakily as she walked back to her chair. He wasn't angry. He hadn't yelled at her!

As Chuck came in with Toby, Libby wished for a secret formula that would make her invisible. It made her feel terrible when Toby tried to break away from Chuck and run from the room.

"We'll have a nice chat," said Chuck, his arm around Toby. "You and I will sit here and Libby can stay right where she is." Chuck sat on his chair and pulled Toby on his lap. Toby buried his face against Chuck's neck.

Libby closed her eyes, wishing she were a million miles away.

"Libby tells me she's very sorry for slapping you, Toby," said Chuck softly. "She feels terrible about it. But Toby, she was upset about her puzzle box missing." He lifted Toby's head away so he could look at his face. Where did you put the puzzle box, Son?"

Libby waited anxiously.

"Nowhere," said Toby barely above a whisper.

"Did you look in her closet at the box?" asked Chuck.

"No," said Toby emphatically. "I didn't take her old box. I didn't touch it. I hate her box and I hate her."

Libby slumped down in the chair.

"Why do you hate her, Toby?" asked Chuck quietly.

"She's mean! She beats me and she takes my food and won't let me have it." Toby was almost shouting.

"Shhhh, Toby. Don't get upset," said Chuck, hugging him close again as he looked over at Libby questioningly.

"I never!" she cried, her hazel eyes wide. "I only slapped him last night, and why would I take his food?"

Chuck patted Toby soothingly. "Toby, you don't want to get Elizabeth in trouble, do you?"

Toby pulled back from Chuck. "She's not Elizabeth. She's Janis!"

"See!" cried Libby, leaping up. "He said it again, Dad. He thinks I'm Janis. He's weird!"

"Sit down, Elizabeth," said Chuck sternly. "I'll handle this." He stood Toby down, facing Libby, his arm firmly about him. "Look at Elizabeth. You've seen her since you've come to live with us. You have no reason to fear her. She's our girl, Elizabeth Gail. I don't know why you think her name is Janis, but you're wrong."

Libby listened hopefully as Chuck reasoned with Toby. Would it help? Who in the world was Janis?

"Toby, I think we'll have to talk about this another time," said Chuck as he stood up. "I want you to tell me once again about the puzzle box, and then you'd better get up to bed."

Toby stood with his thumb in his mouth, his red hair mussed. Finally he pulled his thumb out. "I didn't take the puzzle box. I don't know anything about it."

"All right, Son," said Chuck, squeezing his shoulder. "Up to bed with you. I'll be up later to tuck you in."

Libby sighed unhappily. Nothing was settled. Well, at least she felt better for telling what she'd done.

Toby stopped at the study door and looked right at Libby. "I hope you never find your box, Janis." Then he dashed out, slamming the door.

"If that doesn't beat all," said Chuck, leaning against his desk, his hands on his hips.

"What will we do now?" asked Libby, standing in front of him and looking into his kind face, his brows drawn together over his large nose.

"We'll sure pray about it, Elizabeth. And I think tomorrow I'll call Miss Miller. There might be something written in Toby's case history that will help us solve this." He caught her hands and held them firmly. "Smile, honey. We'll find the answer."

"What about my box?"

"I asked Mom to look for it in Toby's room while I was talking with you both," said Chuck, walking to the study door with her. "We'll ask her what she found."

Libby smiled confidently. Maybe tonight she'd get the box open. Maybe tonight she'd discover the secrets inside the box. Shivers ran up and down her spine. She could hardly wait to get her hands on the shiny box.

They found Vera in the kitchen fixing a cup of tea. She frowned. "I couldn't find it," she said. "I can't imagine where it would be."

"He said he didn't take it," said Chuck as he took another cup from the cupboard.

"But, who else would?" asked Libby in alarm. None of the others would do such a thing!

"We do have a mystery," said Vera, frowning again. "You're sure you didn't put it in a different place?"

"I didn't," said Libby firmly. How could she? Then, she couldn't bear to touch the box. She couldn't think about her real dad. Now, it didn't hurt.

"The kids are in the family room," said Vera, starting toward the door. "Let's ask them."

Libby followed nervously. It would be terrible if one of them had taken it.

"Kids," said Vera, waiting until they looked at her, "Libby's box is missing. Do any of you know where it is?"

In a flash Ben, Susan, and Kevin were surrounding Libby, all talking at once.

"Kids! Kids!" exclaimed Chuck, frowning. "Quiet, please. I can see you don't know where the box is. I think the best thing to do is look around the house just in case Toby did take it and put it down somewhere."

Libby smiled happily, glad that none of them had taken her box. Had she walked in her sleep sometime and moved the box? She would look carefully all around her room.

"The one who finds the box gets to share the secrets inside," said Kevin grinning.

"No way," said Chuck, laughing as he slapped Kevin on the bottom.

Later Libby sat at her desk in her room, the latest letter from her dad in her hands. Should she open it now? She turned it over and over. She felt sad. Would she have loved him if he'd stayed and made a real home for her and Mother?

Slowly she tore open the envelope and pulled out the folded paper. Her heart raced. This was the first letter that she really wanted to read.

Dear Elizabeth Gail, she read aloud, smiling at the now recognized heading and writing.

How are you? Have you opened your secret box? Do you think you could write to me? I enclosed my address inside the box if you would. I do want to hear from you so that I can get to know you.

Libby blinked back tears. He really wanted to know her. But he never would. Maybe it was better that way, then he wouldn't have to discover that he really couldn't love her or want her.

She continued to read.

Old Zeb has heard all about you. We talk about you when we're sitting alone in the evenings. Old Zeb hasn't been well the past few months. It left me with a lot of work on my hands. But I have learned to enjoy working with the cattle.

We have two foals that I take care of. You should see them. One is all black and the other is a palomino. I call them Midnight and Sunlight.

Old Zeb found some coyote pups last winter. We raised them, then took them to the zoo in Lincoln. I had to take them. Old Zeb wouldn't set his foot in a town as big as Lincoln. You would have liked those frisky little pups.

I miss you, Daughter. It had taken me a long time to write these letters to you. Maybe I'll find the courage to write and send letters on my own.

Taped to the bottom of this letter are the directions to opening the secret box. Enjoy the secrets inside.

I love you, Elizabeth Gail. I am proud that you are my daughter. Your father, Frank Dobbs.

Libby laid the letter down with a long, sad sigh. Hot tears stung her eyes. Quickly she wiped them away. It was too late to be sad about her dad.

She wrung her hands in agitation. Where was the box? What secrets were inside? Now that she wanted to know the secrets inside, the box was missing. Would she ever get it back?

THIRTEEN
"Janis" mystery solved

"Miss Miller will be right with you, Mr. Johnson," said the gray-haired woman sitting at the reception desk.

Libby hung back near the door. How well she remembered this place. The gray-haired woman had never liked her. Libby twisted her fingers nervously as she remembered the time the woman had yelled at her and made her sit in the corner until Miss Miller was finished interviewing a new family for Libby.

Libby sighed. She had sat in the corner thirty-five minutes. Before she left she'd pushed all the papers off that woman's desk onto the floor. How angry she'd been!

"Come on, Libby," said Chuck, holding his left hand out to her. Toby was clinging tightly to his right hand.

With mixed feelings Libby walked into Miss Miller's small office. Her huge desk was littered with what she called case histories and paper work concerning all the boys and girls in her charge.

Miss Miller greeted them happily, asking them to be seated. Libby smelled the beautiful perfume as Miss

Miller leaned against her desk, looking from one to another.

"Toby," said Miss Miller, smiling at the red-headed boy sucking his thumb, "I hear you've had the mistaken impression that Libby is someone else. I have been in charge of Libby's care for about five years. I know this girl is Elizabeth Gail Dobbs." Miss Miller smiled at Libby as she pushed her hands down into the pockets of her blue wrap-around skirt.

Libby watched as Toby violently shook his head, then pressed his face against Chuck's jacket sleeve. What would it take to prove to Toby who she was?

Miss Miller walked around her desk and lifted the phone. "Mary, send her in, please."

Libby looked quickly at Chuck. Who was coming in? Surely not Mother! But maybe Miss Miller thought Toby would believe Libby's own mother. Please, please not Mother. Shivers ran up and down Libby's back.

The door opened and a tall, thin girl about fourteen walked in. "What d'ya want now?" she asked, frowning at Miss Miller.

"Look who's here," said Miss Miller, indicating Toby.

The girl looked, then shrugged her shoulders. "What do I care?"

"Toby, look," said Chuck, pulling Toby away and turning him around.

"Janis!" cried Toby, shrinking against Chuck in fright.

Libby gasped. She did look a little like Janis, both of them tall and thin with short, brown hair.

Janis whirled around to Miss Miller, her hands on her hips. "You ain't goin' to put that kid on me again. I got a good home and I don't want him there to ruin it!"

100

"No, Janis," said Miss Miller gently. "You aren't responsible for Toby any longer. He's going to stay with the Johnsons. You may go now. Tell Mrs. Lewis that I'll call her later today." Miss Miller walked around and put her hand on Janis's arm. "Thank you for coming in."

Janis shrugged the hand off, then marched out of the room, her chin in the air.

Libby shook her head in disbelief. Did Toby really think she was like that?

Chuck held Toby firmly by the shoulders. "Is our girl Janis?" he asked softly.

Libby waited as Toby looked her up and down. "I guess not," he said with a frown.

Libby laughed. "I'm Elizabeth Gail Dobbs," said Libby, looking right at Toby. For once he didn't look scared. He even laughed. The others joined in. Libby felt like doing a flip right in Miss Miller's office.

"Toby and Janis had a very hard time," said Miss Miller as she leaned against her desk again. "Janis was too young to have the responsibility for her brother. She beat him and starved him. Libby, if he was frightened of you, it was understandable." Miss Miller looked at Toby. "Toby, you are safe now. The Johnsons are your family, including Libby."

Chuck stood up, his hand on Toby's shoulder. "Thank you, Miss Miller. We appreciate all your help in solving this mystery."

Toby walked right up to Libby and took her hand, tugging her toward the door.

Tears pricked Libby's eyes. It was wonderful that Toby liked her now. He really liked her! She sat with him in the front seat of the car. Coming, she'd had to sit in the back to keep him from getting hysterical.

Libby watched the telephone poles whiz past as Chuck drove them home. She frowned thoughtfully. Toby had only hated her because he thought she was Janis. It had nothing to do with her. It wasn't anything she'd done. Libby rubbed her hands down her skirt. Maybe there was nothing wrong with her.

Grandpa had said that her dad had left her because of something lacking in his life. Was Grandpa right about that? Could it be? Was she as wrong about Dad as she had been about Toby? Toby hadn't feared and hated her because of herself, but because of Janis.

Libby turned to Chuck as he slowed for a curve. "Dad, do you think my real dad left me because I am ugly and acted terrible?"

Chuck looked quickly at her, then back to the road. "Elizabeth, your dad left because *he* couldn't take the responsibility of a family. It had nothing to do with you. It was something lacking in him."

Libby leaned contentedly against the seat, a small smile on her lips. A ton weight seemed to have lifted off her. Finally she was free to love her real dad and accept the fact that he loved her.

When she got home she would open the puzzle box— that is, if the family found it.

FOURTEEN
Secrets

Libby sat next to Susan on the basement floor in front of the brick fireplace. Disappointment over not finding the box after days of searching was finally being replaced by excitement. She shivered in anticipation.

"This will be a plan, the master plan," said Kevin earnestly as he leaned forward and looked from one to another.

"I do think it will work," said Ben, nodding his head up and down. "I really do."

Libby giggled nervously, her heart racing as Toby and Susan agreed. "What do I do first?" asked Libby, locking her fingers around her right knee. Out of all their suggestions, this one sounded like a winner.

"Put the last letter from your dad in your top desk drawer," said Kevin, shoving his glasses back into place.

"Then we'll all spread the word about how excited we are that he sent directions to open the box," said Ben, grinning. "We won't let on that we don't have the box."

"Whoever wanted that box bad enough to take it will

try to take the directions," said Susan, her red-gold ponytails bobbing wildly. "Then, we'll catch him!"

"I'm glad I get a turn to watch Libby's room," said Toby, smiling happily. He wasn't sucking his thumb. He hadn't for the past three days. Well, maybe only when he was overtired.

"Remember this," said Ben earnestly. "If anyone asks to come over to play, say no at first. If they get desperate, then agree to have them over."

"I sure hope it doesn't take long to trap the enemy," said Libby. "I want to see what's in my box."

"We all do," said Susan excitely. She touched Libby's arm. "Don't you worry, Libby. We've prayed that we'd find your box, and we came up with this fantastic plan." She nodded her head, looking very smug. "We'll get the box back."

What if the box had already been opened, the secrets discovered? No! She wouldn't even think that.

Ben laid a pad of paper on his knee and poised a short pencil over it. "We'll write the schedule for guarding Libby's room. Who wants first watch?"

A few days later Libby, Susan, and Ben galloped along the path in the back of the farm buildings. Libby knew Toby was on watch.

The sun felt good on Libby's bare head. What a beautiful warm day for March!

Libby reined in Tessy as she neared the farm buildings. Her bedroom window was in full view. A movement in her room caught her attention. Libby shivered as she stopped Tessy. Toby was on watch. Was he in her room? She turned as the others stopped beside her. "Ben! Susan! Someone's in my room. Let's hurry!"

The warm wind whipped her hair back as Tessy galloped to the yard, Apache Girl and Star right behind.

Libby slid off Tessy and handed Susan the reins. "I'll go check." Her heart raced as she dashed upstairs. Noise from her room sent her heart zooming. She took a deep breath, then slowly let it out. With shaking hands she opened her bedroom door wide. Brenda and Toby were tussling frantically.

"I caught her," cried Toby, hanging on for dear life, his face glowing with pride. Blood was oozing from a scratch on his left cheek. "She had your letter in her jacket pocket."

"Liar!" cried Brenda, jerking free at last, her eyes wild as she tried to find a way to escape.

"I'll handle her now, Toby," said Libby grimly. "Let's go get my box." She stepped close to Brenda, her eyes narrowed.

Brenda shrank back. "Don't hit me!"

"I won't if you give back my box." Libby clenched her fists at her sides. For some reason she didn't even desire to hit Brenda. Just to know she'd have her box back soon made her feel good. To think that God answered another prayer for her! She smiled at the thought. "Come on, Brenda," said Libby, trying not to be cheerful. "Let's get my box."

"Don't forget the letter in her pocket," said Toby, prancing around the room excitedly.

Libby pulled the letter out of Brenda's pocket and stuck it back in her desk drawer. Soon, soon she'd have her box! "Come on, Brenda. Let's go."

Toby followed them out, grabbing his coat.

The others met her at the back door. Noisily they walked down the road to the Wilkens house. Joe opened the door in surprise.

"What have you done now, Brenda?" asked Joe, flushing with embarrassment, and looking at the Johnson kids and his sister.

"She has my box," said Libby, finally releasing Brenda's arm. "Get it, Brenda."

"Oh, Brenda!" cried Joe, staring at her unhappily. "How could you, after you promised Mom there'd be no more trouble!"

"Shut up, Joe!" screamed Brenda, her dark eyes blazing.

"We're waiting, Brenda," said Susan coldly.

They trooped after Brenda to her room. Ungraciously, Brenda shoved the box into Libby's arms.

"I hate you, aid kid," hissed Brenda. "I hope your box is completely empty."

Libby smiled down at her box, holding it tightly against her chest. Brenda's fingerprints dulled the finish on the box. At least she hadn't opened it. Happiness flooded over her. She didn't even hate Brenda.

"Want to come home with us and watch me open the box?" asked Libby, looking from Joe to Brenda.

Brenda gasped in surprise as Joe excitedly agreed.

"I know you want to see what's inside, Brenda," said Libby. "So come home with us." It felt great not hating Brenda.

Brenda hesitated, then jerked her jacket off. "I wouldn't come to your house to watch you open your stupid box if you forced me! I don't care what's in it." She stood stiffly beside her bed. "Now, get out of my room and out of my house!"

Libby turned and walked out, the others behind her. How good it felt to hold the box from her own dad. What was inside? What?

106

A few minutes later they clustered around Libby in the family room, everyone talking at once.

"Quiet," demanded Ben, frowning. "Let's all be quiet and watch Libby open the box."

"Try to open it without the directions," said Susan excitedly.

Lovingly, Libby rubbed the box off with a soft cloth. Once again it shone brightly. "I'll try," she whispered. Gently she slid out a combination of pieces. Nothing happened.

"I can't stand this," said Kevin, groaning as he pulled his hair. "Read the directions and open the box!"

With trembling fingers Libby spread the directions on the floor and tried to read them as the others pressed in close. She licked her dry lips.

Finally she pulled out the secret drawer. As she did, the top popped up, revealing another compartment. Libby closed her eyes and covered her heart. She took a deep breath. "Call Mom and Dad," she whispered hoarsely. She wanted them to be there as she opened the secrets.

Everyone was completely silent as Ben hurried after Vera. The grandfather clock bonged five, startling Libby. Chuck wouldn't be home for another hour. She couldn't wait that long.

When Vera was seated on the blue chair behind her, Libby slowly lifted out the paper on top. It was a note in Frank Dobbs' handwriting.

"Please, please hurry," said Susan in agony. "I can't stand this!"

Elizabeth Gail, read Libby, the note shaking so she could hardly read it. She forced her hand to be steady. *I'm glad you've opened the box. See the small envelope in the top part of the box? Open it first, honey.*

"I'm going to die!" cried Susan, pretending to faint. Then she popped back up as Libby pulled a photograph out of the envelope.

Libby blinked back tears as she looked at the man and baby. She turned it over and read, "Frank and

Elizabeth." She studied the picture closer. She looked like Dad, she really did. Without a word she handed the picture to Vera, then Vera handed it around.

"What next?" asked Toby, rocking back and forth excitedly.

Libby continued to read. *Next, open the small box. This I bought for your tenth birthday, hoping I'd find the courage to visit you.*

Libby tore the paper off the small box. This was better than any Christmas, any birthday she'd ever had.

"It's a necklace," said Susan as Libby held up the silver chain, two hearts locked together swinging from it.

"It's lovely," said Vera, hooking it around Libby's slender neck.

Libby fingered it lovingly. Dad really had thought of her!

"Hurry, hurry, Libby," begged Kevin, his eyes big and round behind his glasses.

Libby found her place in the note. *Open the tiny square box now. The ring inside is your mother's school ring. She gave it to me when she was sixteen and I eighteen. I've worn it on my little finger all these years. I want you to have it. If it won't fit now, save it until it does, then wear it and think of me.*

Libby blinked back tears as she opened the tiny box. She lifted the ring out and slipped it on the ring finger of her right hand. It was made of white gold and had a large L and a faded date on the crest.

"Let me see it," said Toby, grabbing Libby's hand.

Proudly Libby held her hand out first to one and then another until everyone had seen the ring.

"What wonderful secrets!" exclaimed Vera, brushing tears from her eyes.

Libby blinked hard until she could see to read the rest of the note. *Elizabeth, open the long envelope on the bottom of the drawer. I hope you like everything that I put inside your box. Love, Dad.*

Clumsily Libby tore open the long envelope. She pulled out three pages. One had her father's address in care of Old Zeb on it; another was a letter, and the last a legal paper.

"What is it, Mom?" asked Libby, handing it to her.

"It's a deed to some property in Nebraska," said Vera excitedly, reading the specific location.

"That's part of Old Zeb's ranch," said Ben, his eyes wide. "Libby, you own part of a ranch!"

"Wow!" whispered Susan, clasping her hands over her heart. "Wow!"

Libby swallowed hard. Could it be true?

"Hurry, hurry. Read the letter," said Kevin, thumping Libby's knee.

"I'm sure glad I got to come over to watch this," said Joe, grinning. "Brenda doesn't know what she's missing."

The letter crackled as Libby unfolded it.

Dear Elizabeth Gail.

Libby blinked back tears.

The title to the property gives you legal right to it. Old Zeb gave me a house and three hundred acres. It is the only thing of value I've ever owned. I want you to have it. I'll live with Old Zeb and take care of his ranch and yours. Someday maybe I'll find the courage to bring you here.

Elizabeth, you are more important to me than the

*property. You are more important to me than my own
life. I want you to write to me. If you want to, that is. I
will always love you. Maybe we'll meet soon. Love, Dad.*

Tears streamed down Libby's cheeks as she hugged
the letter to her heart and rocked back and forth.

Libby suddenly noticed Chuck standing in the door-
way. His strong arms gathered her close. Libby buried
her face against Chuck's chest and cried uncontrollably. His hands were still cold from being outdoors.

Finally she pulled away from him and blew her nose
and wiped her eyes.

"Your dad gave you part of himself," said Chuck as
he looked at the "secrets." "Now you can remember
him with love."

"I'm glad," said Libby, her eyes sparkling. She
smiled, then kissed Chuck.

"Dad, when can we visit Libby's ranch?" asked
Kevin, grabbing Chuck's hand?

"When, Dad?" asked Susan and Toby together.

"What do you think, Vera?" asked Chuck, putting his
arm around her waist. "Would you like to visit the
sandhills of Nebraska?"

Vera laughed. "I think we all would."

"I wish the Johnson family would adopt me," said
Joe wistfully. "I'd like to see the ranch, too." He poked
his hands into his jeans pockets and twisted his toe in
the thick carpet.

"Maybe we can arrange something," said Chuck
happily.

"What if Brenda asks to go?" whispered Susan just
for Libby to hear. "Wouldn't that spoil everything?"

"It sure would," said Libby. Then, she remembered
how many prayers the Lord had answered. Maybe he

would change Brenda so that they could all love her. "Maybe it wouldn't be so bad, Susan."

Susan shrugged. "Maybe."

"Listen, kids," said Chuck, turning to each of them. "This would be a very good time to say thank you to God."

"May I take my turn to pray?" asked Libby as she held out one hand to Susan and the other to Joe.

Hand in hand in a circle they all bowed their heads. Libby felt as if she would burst with joy as she prayed. She thanked God for changing her and taking away the hate and bitterness she had harbored in her heart toward her real dad.

Later she looked at each of them. She had the best family in the world. The very best.

"Dad," said Toby, grabbing Chuck's hand, "when can we visit Libby's ranch?"

Suddenly it seemed very real to Libby. She owned a ranch! "When, Dad?" she asked, grabbing his other hand.

"We have a vacation in June," said Chuck. "How would that be?"

Libby flung her arms around him. Only three months away! Then she was crushed as everyone tried to hug Dad at once.